Space Cadet Legacy

in

"Princess Lydia and the Eldergreen Boundary"

Book #38 in the Space Cadet Richard Series

Russell Vance McFall

This is a work of fiction. Names, characters, places, and incidents are either products of the author's imagination or used fictitiously. Any resemblance to actual persons, living or dead, or actual events is purely coincidental.

Published by Ordained Path Books
For permissions or inquiries, contact:
ordainedpathbooks@gmail.com

Cover illustration and interior artwork generated by AI under direction of the author.

First Edition.

*"Your word is a lamp to my feet
And a light to my path."*
—Psalm 119:105 (NASB)

Ordained Path Books is dedicated to stories that reflect timeless truths, courage, and the quiet strength of faith—guided by purpose, and written to inspire the next generation.

ISBN (Paperback): 978-1-972724-08-8
ISBN (Hardcover): 978-1-972724-11-8

Printed in the United States of America.

Version 1.02 -- April 2026

Dedication

For my niece,
who reminds me why these stories are worth telling—
and who continues to believe that exploring the unknown
is always worth the journey.

About the Emblem — Delta Directive

The Delta Emblem is not a symbol of authority.
It is a reminder of responsibility.

At its center is a triangle, representing the three virtues that make the Delta Directive possible:

Integrity — truth held even when unseen.
Unity — trust shared among the team.
Discretion — restraint exercised without recognition.

Remove any one of these, and trust does not fail loudly.
It erodes quietly.

Beneath the triangle are four stars, representing the cadets entrusted with the Directive. The stars are placed below the triangle to remind them that character must rest on something greater than individual achievement.

The emblem carries no weapons, no rank, and no symbols of force.
It does not grant authority.
It marks a commitment.

In this mission, that commitment is tested in a different way.
Not by what must be done—
but by what must be left undone.

Delta is not about power.
It is about choosing what must be protected—
and carrying that responsibility without applause.

Cast of Characters

Richard Taylor

Commanding officer of the Delta team. Calm, disciplined, and attentive to timing and context, Richard leads through restraint rather than force. He carries responsibility even when outcomes cannot be fully measured or explained, and understands that success is not always defined by what is taken—but by what is handled correctly.

Ashton Quinn

Operations and systems specialist. Ashton excels at recognizing patterns that emerge indirectly rather than directly. She combines analytical precision with quiet insight, often identifying when a system is reacting to its environment rather than functioning within it.

Dooley Lewis

Engineering and systems integration lead. Practical, precise, and dependable, Dooley stabilizes complex situations with measured action and careful adjustment. His steady presence supports the team's ability to act without overcorrecting.

Milo Santiago

Data and environmental analysis specialist. Younger than the rest of the team but highly focused, Milo observes subtle changes in terrain, movement, and alignment—often identifying patterns before they are fully visible to others.

Allied Personnel

Princess Lydia

Guide to the Eldergreen Expanse and daughter of the ruling authority. Lydia understands the forest not as a place to move through, but as a system to be read. Her leadership reflects patience, awareness, and the discipline required to enter a place correctly rather than force a path through it.

Serana

Royal guardian assigned to Princess Lydia. Highly trained, observant, and disciplined, Serana operates with constant awareness of risk. She evaluates situations without overreaction, ensuring safety through control rather than escalation.

Mission-Related Personnel

Kael Thorn

Independent operator who transported the Quantum StarPath Core into the Eldergreen Expanse. Capable and determined, he reached the objective but failed to fully understand the system he was handling or the environment he entered. His outcome serves as a reminder that reaching a destination is not the same as returning from it.

Command & Oversight

Admiral Jack Taylor

Senior Earth Command officer overseeing mission execution. Provides clear direction while allowing the Delta team to operate within their own judgment, trusting their ability to act with restraint and precision.

Calvinius Calhoun

Senior authority connected to Delta operations. Calvinius operates above standard command structure, guiding missions that require discretion, trust, and careful judgment rather than visible intervention.

President Dash Lincoln

President of United Earth. Engages quietly in matters where responsibility matters more than recognition. His leadership reflects trust, restraint, and the importance of decisions made without public visibility.

Support Systems

Mother

The AI aboard the Delta-assigned vessel. Mother monitors and executes operations strictly within defined parameters. She does not speculate or interpret beyond system tolerances and records no anomaly unless one can be measured.

Whizzy

A small spherical support AI with a single central eye and retractable limbs. Whizzy observes quietly and detects subtle structural details others may overlook. Intervention is rare—but always timely.

Guiding Framework

The Delta Directive

Not a character, but the guiding principle behind all Delta operations. The Directive represents responsibility without recognition, authority without force, and the discipline to act—or not act—based on what preserves the greater outcome.

Contents

Prologue — The Thief's Flight

The corridor lights dimmed twice before stabilizing.

Kael Thorn noticed.

He always noticed things like that.

A flicker in the power grid. A delay in a door cycle. A hum that sounded just a little too uneven. Years of working as a navigation technician had trained him to pay attention to the small details—the quiet warnings that most people ignored.

Tonight, those details mattered more than ever.

He stood just outside the secured access hatch, one hand resting lightly against the cool metal wall, his breathing steady but shallow. The corridor beyond was empty, stretching in both directions with the polished stillness of a place designed to look safe.

It wasn't safe.

Not for him.

Kael glanced once over his shoulder. No footsteps. No voices. Just the faint mechanical rhythm of the station breathing around him.

He turned back to the hatch.

"Last chance," he muttered under his breath.

He paused.

"Keep the systems warm," he said quietly, not turning.

The response came through his comm a second later.

"They've been warm," a younger voice replied. "You just make sure you come back."

His fingers moved quickly across the panel, entering a code he had no business knowing. The system hesitated—a fraction of a second too long—then the lock disengaged with a soft click.

Kael exhaled slowly.

"Good," he whispered. "Still works."

The hatch slid open.

Inside, the room was smaller than he expected. Clean. Controlled. Quiet in a way that felt almost unnatural. The kind of quiet that came from systems designed never to fail.

At the center of the room, suspended within a transparent containment frame, was the device.

The Quantum StarPath Core.

Kael had seen one before, years ago, from a distance, during a routine calibration job on a long-range transport vessel. Even then, it had felt important—like standing near something that quietly held the fate of entire journeys in its calculations.

Now he was standing right in front of one.

Up close, it was heavier than he remembered. Not just in weight, but in presence. The core was housed in a compact, reinforced casing, its surface etched with faint lines that pulsed with a soft, shifting glow. Inside, layers of crystalline arrays rotated slowly, adjusting themselves in response to gravitational data streaming from systems far beyond the station.

It was beautiful.

And it did not belong to him.

Kael hesitated.

For just a moment, the room seemed to press in around him, the quiet growing louder in his ears. He could walk away. Close the hatch. Pretend he had never been here.

He thought of the debts.

Of the messages that had stopped sounding like requests and started sounding like warnings.

Of the last conversation, where the man on the other end hadn't bothered to hide what would happen if Kael didn't find a way to pay.

His jaw tightened.

"Too late for that," he said softly.

He stepped forward.

The containment field shimmered as he reached in, tools already in his hand. He worked quickly, efficiently, the way he always had when systems needed to be bypassed without drawing attention. One panel released. Then another. The field flickered, recalibrated, then dropped entirely.

The room remained silent.

Kael lifted the Core.

It was heavier than it looked—dense, compact, solid in a way that forced him to adjust his grip. Forty pounds, maybe a little more. Manageable, but not something you wanted to carry far.

He secured it against his chest.

"Alright," he said, forcing a breath. "That's done."

"Then move," the voice said. "Power draw just spiked. They're going to see it."

A soft tone sounded behind him.

Not loud.

Not urgent.

But wrong.

Kael turned.

The access panel outside the room had shifted from green to amber.

His stomach dropped.

"No, no… come on…"

Another tone followed, slightly sharper this time.

The system had noticed.

Of course it had noticed.

He moved fast.

The hatch slid open just as the corridor lights brightened, the station responding to the change in status. Somewhere deeper in the system, protocols were waking up—quiet ones at first, designed to verify, to confirm, to double-check.

That gave him seconds.

Maybe.

Kael stepped into the corridor and turned left, moving quickly but not running. Running would draw attention. Running would confirm what the system was already beginning to suspect.

"Stay calm," he muttered. "Just another tech doing his job."

Another tone.

Louder this time.

The amber light shifted toward red.

"Alright, that's not good," he said.

He broke into a run.

The Core shifted in his arms as he moved, forcing him to tighten his grip. It wasn't designed for this—for being carried through corridors by someone who had just stolen it. It was meant to sit in a controlled environment, calculating safe paths through space, guiding ships across distances no human could comprehend.

Now it was a liability.

A very heavy one.

Kael reached the end of the corridor and turned sharply, nearly colliding with a maintenance cart. He caught himself, steadied the Core, and kept moving.

Behind him, the first alarm sounded.

Not loud enough to cause panic.

But loud enough to mean this was no longer contained.

"They're early," he said, breath quickening. "That's… that's fine. I can still—"

He didn't finish the sentence.

Because he knew he was lying.

The ship was exactly where he had left it.

And exactly where it needed to be.

Docked at the far edge of the station, tucked into a maintenance bay that rarely saw traffic. It wasn't much to look at—patched panels, mismatched plating, systems that worked just well enough to pass inspection if no one looked too closely.

It would have to do.

Kael crossed the bay at a half-run, the alarm now echoing faintly through the structure behind him. He reached the access ramp, paused just long enough to catch his breath, then hurried inside.

"Took you long enough," the younger man said from the pilot's seat.

Kael didn't answer right away. He just set the Core down and exhaled.

"Let's go," he said.

The interior lights flickered as he entered.

"Yeah, yeah, I know," he muttered, setting the Core down carefully near the navigation console. "You don't like surprises either."

He moved to the pilot's seat and powered up the systems. The ship responded slowly, as if waking from a deep sleep it hadn't been ready to leave.

"Come on," Kael said, tapping the console. "We don't have time for this today."

The engines hummed to life.

Outside, the bay doors began to open.

Kael glanced at the Core.

For a moment, just a moment, he allowed himself to think that maybe this would work. That he would get clear, find a buyer, pay off the debt, and disappear somewhere quiet where no one would ever look for him again.

"Simple," he said. "In and out."

"It was never going to be simple," the younger man said quietly.

The ship lurched as it cleared the docking clamps.

Then everything went wrong.

The navigation display flickered.

Coordinates shifted.

Warnings began to populate the screen faster than he could read them.

Kael frowned.

"That's… that's not right."

He reached over and adjusted the interface, linking the ship's navigation system directly to the Core. If anything could stabilize the calculations, it would be that.

The Core responded.

Its internal arrays spun faster, the soft glow intensifying as it processed the incoming data.

For a second, the readings stabilized.

Then they didn't.

The display warped, the projected route bending in ways that made no sense.

"Hey," Kael said, leaning forward. "No, no, no… you don't get to do that."

He tapped commands into the console, trying to override the instability.

The Core pulsed again.

Stronger this time.

The ship shuddered.

Kael froze.

"That's not supposed to happen," he whispered.

The alarms changed.

Different now.

Not security.

System failure.

"Alright," he said quickly. "We can fix this. We've fixed worse than this."

He hadn't.

Not like this.

The ship surged forward, clearing the station's perimeter and entering open space. Kael grabbed the controls, fighting to keep the vessel steady as the navigation system struggled to reconcile the Core's calculations with the ship's outdated hardware.

"Come on… just hold together…"

The stars ahead stretched.

Not in the smooth, controlled way of a proper jump.

This was uneven.

Unstable.

Wrong.

Kael's hands tightened on the controls.

"Okay," he said, voice rising despite himself. "New plan. We're not jumping. We are definitely not—"

The Core flared with light.

The ship lurched violently.

And the stars disappeared.

When they came back, everything was on fire.

Not literally.

Not yet.

But the readouts might as well have been.

"Atmospheric entry detected."

"What?" Kael snapped, eyes darting across the displays. "No, no, no, we're not anywhere near—"

The external sensors struggled to keep up as the ship slammed into the upper layers of an atmosphere it had never planned to enter.

Friction built instantly.

Heat surged across the hull.

Kael fought the controls, trying to level the descent, but the ship responded sluggishly, as if every system was arguing with every other system at once.

"Stabilize," he said through clenched teeth. "Just stabilize—"

The ship rolled.

Hard.

The viewport filled with a blur of green and gold.

Forest.

Endless forest.

"Of all the places…" he muttered.

Warnings flooded the console.

Hull stress.

Engine imbalance.

Navigation failure.

"Yeah, I got it," he said, gripping the controls tighter. "You don't have to list them all."

The ship dropped lower, breaking through the canopy in a violent cascade of snapping branches and splintering wood. Kael braced himself as the vessel slammed into the ground, skidding through dense undergrowth before finally coming to a grinding, jarring halt.

Silence followed.

Heavy.

Absolute.

Kael didn't move at first.

Then he inhaled sharply and let the breath out in a shaky laugh.

"Still here," he said. "That's… that's something."

He glanced at the Core.

It still glowed.

Steady.

Unbothered.

"Of course you're fine," he said. "Why wouldn't you be fine?"

Outside, the forest stretched in every direction.

Dense.

Unfamiliar.

Alive in a way that made the air itself feel different.

Kael swallowed.

"Alright," he said quietly. "Now what?"

He didn't have an answer.

And somewhere, far off in the distance, something moved.

Chapter 1 — The Call to Report

Morning drills had ended an hour ago, but the training deck still carried the after-feel of motion.

The air smelled faintly of warmed metal, recycled air, and the rubberized flooring used for impact work. Across the wide compartment, a few cadets were finishing cooldown laps while others wiped down equipment or traded tired remarks about instructors who always seemed to believe one more round would somehow fix every weakness in the known universe.

Richard Taylor leaned against the padded wall near the edge of the deck and took a long drink from his water bottle. Sweat still clung to the back of his neck, but his breathing had already settled. He had never been the loudest one in training, never the one trying hardest to impress people watching from the sidelines. He simply worked. Steady. Consistent. The kind of effort that rarely drew applause but usually got noticed anyway.

A practice baton struck the floor nearby with a hollow clack.

Dooley Lewis looked down at it, frowned, and then bent to pick it up with exaggerated dignity.

"I meant to do that," he announced.

No one believed him.

Ashton Quinn, sitting cross-legged on a supply crate while tightening a strap on one of her boots, didn't even bother looking up. "If by 'meant to do that' you mean 'lost your grip because you were talking while spinning,' then yes. Extremely intentional."

Dooley pointed the baton at her. "You always remove the poetry from my best moments."

"I remove the fiction."

"It was one mistake."

"It was three mistakes connected by momentum."

That made Milo Santiago smile, though only slightly. He sat on the floor near the wall with his back against a folded training mat, one knee drawn up, quietly rewrapping the tape around his right wrist. Milo did most things quietly. Even at rest he had a way of making himself smaller than the space around him, as if he never wanted to be the reason attention shifted in his direction. But he missed very little. His eyes moved from Dooley to Ashton to Richard and back again, taking in tone and posture and all the little signs that told him where the mood of the room was headed.

Dooley dropped down beside him with a groan.

"I think Captain Dorn was trying to kill us today."

Milo glanced sideways. "You say that every time."

"Because every time it feels more likely."

Richard capped his bottle and walked over. "You did fine."

Dooley looked up at him. "That is a very responsible thing to say while avoiding the truth."

"The truth is you talk during drills."

"The truth," Ashton said, standing now, "is that you try to turn everything into a dramatic story while your feet are still moving."

Dooley gave her a wounded look. "I bring personality to the team."

"You bring noise to the team."

"I bring morale."

Ashton shrugged. "That part is true."

Richard let the corner of his mouth lift. It was a familiar rhythm with them now. Ashton's dry observations, Dooley's relentless optimism, Milo's quiet watchfulness. Together they made a kind of balance that somehow worked better than it should have. None of them would have put it that way out loud, but Richard had begun to understand that teams were often built as much from temperament as from skill.

He glanced toward the far end of the deck where a wall display still listed the day's schedule. The rest of the afternoon looked routine enough—equipment inspection, navigation review, evening study block. Nothing unusual.

For once.

That thought had barely crossed his mind when the overhead chime sounded.

Not the general tone used for announcements.

A single, clear note.

Then a second.

Several cadets across the room slowed or turned. On the wall display, the training schedule vanished and was replaced by a line of text.

CADETS R. TAYLOR, A. QUINN, D. LEWIS, M. SANTIAGO — REPORT TO COMMAND BRIEFING ROOM THREE IMMEDIATELY.

For a second, no one moved.

Dooley was the first to speak.

"Well," he said, "that can't be bad."

Ashton looked at him. "You say that like someone who has never heard the word immediately before."

"It could still be good."

"It is never good when the message sounds like it was written by a wall."

Richard was already straightening. The easy mood that had lingered after training seemed to drain quietly out of the room. Not because the summons sounded angry. It didn't. If anything, it sounded too neutral for that. But cadets were not called to a command briefing room in the middle of an otherwise normal day without a reason.

Milo stood and finished adjusting the tape on his wrist. "Did we miss something?"

"I don't think so," Richard said.

Ashton slung one booted foot down from the crate and pulled the other snug. "That's not especially comforting."

Dooley rose more slowly. "Do you think we're in trouble?"

Ashton gave him a flat look. "Are you asking from a place of innocence, or are you trying to remember something you forgot to tell us?"

"I am asking from a place of deep concern and limited information."

"That means yes," she said.

Richard picked up his jacket from the bench and shrugged into it. "Let's not invent problems before we get there."

Dooley brightened slightly. "That sounds wise and hopeful."

"It's neither," Ashton said. "It's practical."

Richard checked the display once more, as if expecting further explanation to appear. None did.

He looked at the others. "Come on."

They crossed the deck together.

Conversations around them had already resumed, but differently now. A few curious glances followed them as they passed through the exit hatch and into the corridor beyond. The station's main training level was always busy at this hour, full of cadets moving between assignments, instructors reviewing performance logs, maintenance crews threading their way through everything with expressionless patience. But Richard was more aware of the place now than he had been five minutes earlier. The hum of the ventilation system. The low thrum beneath the deck plating. The polished gray of the walls broken at intervals by viewing ports and status displays. All of it seemed sharper when he didn't know what waited ahead.

Dooley walked with his hands tucked halfway into his jacket pockets.

"So," he said, after they had gone several yards in silence, "I'd like to formally present a list of possible reasons we have been summoned."

"No," Ashton said immediately.

"You haven't even heard them."

"I don't need to."

"What if they're excellent?"

"They won't be."

Dooley ignored her. "Possibility one: special assignment."

"That one I'll allow," Richard said.

Dooley nodded as if grateful for mature leadership. "Possibility two: we're being reassigned to some highly classified mission because someone finally noticed our exceptional qualities."

Ashton made a quiet sound that suggested deep personal doubt.

"Possibility three," Dooley continued, "one of us has unknowingly impressed an important officer."

"This is somehow your least believable theory," Ashton said.

"I am trying to keep morale up."

"You are trying to narrate your own suspense."

"It helps me think."

Milo, walking slightly behind them, said, "Could be mission review."

Richard glanced back. "From what?"

Milo gave a small shrug. "I don't know."

That was Milo sometimes. He rarely pushed his thoughts to the front of a conversation, but when he spoke, it was usually because he had noticed something others had not. Richard slowed just enough to match his pace.

"Something feel off to you?"

Milo hesitated. "Not off exactly. Just… it doesn't sound like a correction meeting."

Ashton looked over at him. "Why?"

"Because they named all four of us together."

That hung in the air for a moment.

Richard considered it and found that Milo was right. Disciplinary matters were usually more specific. Performance reviews too. If this had to do with one mistake, one failed task, one issue with training logs, it likely would not involve the four of them together unless the matter had begun together.

Or unless it was something else entirely.

The corridor curved left, opening into a wider transit hub where several levels connected by stairs and lift shafts. Through the tall forward viewport, space stretched out beyond the station in a black field scattered with hard white stars. A transport shuttle moved slowly away from one docking ring while a supply tender drifted into alignment at another. Far below, the planet filled a third of the view, blue and white and cloud-bound, serene from this distance in a way that always made Richard pause, even when he didn't mean to.

Today he only glanced.

Their destination lay up one level and across the command tier, where the corridors grew quieter and the markings on the walls became more formal. Fewer cadets moved there. More officers. More closed doors.

Dooley dropped his voice as they approached the stairwell. "Alright, serious question. Are we walking too fast? I feel like if we arrive breathing hard it will look suspicious."

Ashton took the first stair. "Suspicious of what?"

"I don't know. Something disorganized."

"You are something disorganized."

Dooley looked to Richard. "See what I endure?"

Richard started up the stairs. "You'll survive."

"Emotionally? Hard to say."

Milo followed with the faintest shake of his head.

They reached the upper landing and continued down a narrower corridor lined with framed mission photographs and plaques marking older expeditions. Richard had passed this way many times, but only occasionally with purpose. Most cadets did. The command tier had a way of making young people stand a little straighter even when no one told them to.

At the far end, a set of double doors marked **BRIEFING ROOM THREE** stood closed beneath a slim overhead light.

No one spoke for a moment.

Dooley finally exhaled. "This somehow looks more official than I hoped."

"It is a briefing room," Ashton said. "Official is the whole point."

Richard slowed as they approached the doors. Through the narrow glass inset he could see movement inside, but not enough to make out clearly who was there. He adjusted his jacket unconsciously, then stopped himself. There was no reason to fidget.

He looked at the others.

Ashton looked composed, though her eyes were more alert than usual. Dooley was trying very hard to look casual and succeeding only in part. Milo had that quiet stillness he sometimes wore when he was listening inwardly as much as outwardly, as though bracing himself not for fear but for information.

Richard rested a hand on the door control.

"Whatever this is," he said quietly, "let's just listen first."

Dooley nodded. "That sounds like the kind of thing people say right before hearing something life-changing."

Ashton folded her arms. "Or paperwork-related."

"Those are not equal possibilities."

"They are until proven otherwise."

Richard pressed the control.

The doors slid open.

The room beyond was cool, bright, and far less crowded than he had expected. A long curved briefing table occupied the center, its surface alive with dark inactive displays waiting to be engaged. A large wall screen filled the far end of the room, currently blank except for a simple command seal. Light from the side viewport washed part of the polished floor in a pale glow.

Only three people were inside.

The first was Admiral Jack Taylor.

Richard noticed him before anything else—not because the admiral was trying to dominate the room, but because he never needed to. He stood near the head of the table with the unforced steadiness of someone accustomed to command and uninterested in displaying it theatrically. His uniform was immaculate, his expression composed, but there was something in the set of his shoulders that suggested this was no routine errand.

Beside him stood Commander Hale from Operations, holding a thin data slate. Near the wall display was a civilian man Richard did not recognize—older, narrow-faced, with tired eyes and the posture of someone who had been carrying too much worry for too long.

The admiral looked up as the four cadets entered.

"Cadets," he said. "Come in."

All four straightened immediately.

Richard felt the shift inside himself then, the final quiet click from uncertainty into attention. Whatever this was, it was real. Not hallway rumor. Not speculation. Not some instructor's surprise review.

Something had happened.

And somehow, they had just stepped into it.

The doors closed softly behind them.

Admiral Taylor gestured toward the near side of the table. "Take your seats."

Richard moved first, the others following. No one spoke as they sat. The room seemed very still now, the kind of stillness that gathered before important information was set loose.

Commander Hale set the data slate onto the table and stepped back.

The civilian man remained standing.

Admiral Taylor looked at each of them in turn before speaking.

"Before we begin," he said, "there is one point of structure that needs to be made clear."

The cadets remained still.

"Delta Team remains under its present authority by direction of the President and Calvinius Calhoune. This assignment comes through that channel."

A brief pause followed—not long, but enough to let the meaning settle.

"For the duration of this mission, however, you will operate in temporary coordination with my command. The diplomatic and operational requirements involved make that necessary."

Richard felt the shift immediately. This was not a routine assignment. If Calvinius had routed it here personally, then whatever followed carried weight beyond a standard retrieval.

Admiral Taylor continued.

"What you are about to hear," he said, "concerns a theft, a crash, a protected planetary territory, and a retrieval problem that has become more complicated than anyone prefers."

Dooley, to his credit, did not say a word.

The admiral continued.

"An advanced navigational device was stolen three months ago from a secured transit facility. At first, authorities believed the thief intended to move it off-market through one of the usual channels. That did not happen. The suspect disappeared, along with the device, and the search widened."

He touched the table surface.

The wall display came alive.

A rotating image appeared above the center of the table—a compact piece of technology housed within a reinforced casing, its inner crystalline structures glowing faintly as they turned in layered synchronization.

Even Ashton leaned forward slightly.

"This," said Admiral Taylor, "is a Quantum StarPath Core."

The device hovered in light between them, quiet and elegant and clearly important.

Richard said nothing, but he understood at once that this was not ordinary equipment.

Commander Hale picked up the explanation. "A StarPath Core processes gravitational drift, dark-current variance, and deep-route stability for long-range navigation. In simple terms, it helps ships avoid dying in very expensive and unpleasant ways."

That sounded like Ashton's kind of explanation. Richard saw her eyes flick briefly toward the commander, as if acknowledging the effort.

"Without one?" Milo asked quietly.

"Without one," Hale said, "certain classes of vessels lose access to the safest route calculations available. Not every ship uses one, but the ones that do depend on them heavily."

The civilian man spoke for the first time. His voice carried the weariness Richard had already seen in his face.

"I oversee logistics security for the station where it was taken. The theft should not have been possible." He looked briefly at the image, then away. "And yet here we are."

Admiral Taylor let that settle a moment.

"The thief's name is Kael Thorn," he said. "Former navigation technician. Skilled enough to know what he was stealing. Desperate enough to try."

Another touch, and the display shifted.

Kael's face appeared beside the hovering image of the Core. Lean face. Sharp eyes. Not a hardened criminal exactly. More like a man who had made too many bad decisions and finally run out of room.

"He escaped in an aging courier ship," the admiral said. "The working theory is that he attempted to integrate the stolen Core into his vessel's failing navigation system."

Ashton spoke before anyone else could. "That's reckless."

"Yes," said Admiral Taylor. "It was."

The wall display changed again.

This time the image showed a planet.

Green dominated almost an entire hemisphere. Vast forest belts spread across the surface in deep layered bands, broken by mountain ridges, rivers, and a scattering of bright coastal settlements. One region in particular expanded as the display zoomed inward—a sweeping forest mass so broad and thick it looked less like terrain and more like weather frozen into land.

"This is Elyndor," the admiral said. "A world under allied governance, environmentally stable, culturally complex, and not especially forgiving to outsiders who assume ignorance can substitute for permission."

Dooley blinked. "That sounds specific."

Admiral Taylor's expression did not change. "It is."

A faint shift went through the room. Not humor exactly. But enough to release some of the tension without breaking it.

Commander Hale stepped forward again. "Kael Thorn's ship entered Elyndor's atmosphere and crashed near the boundary of a heavily protected forest preserve on the planet's eastern hemisphere. He survived the crash. The Core did too."

"The preserve," Admiral Taylor said, "is ancient, legally restricted, ecologically delicate, and partially inhabited by indigenous tribal groups whose territorial protections are recognized by the local monarchy and by interstellar treaty. Entry is tightly controlled."

Ashton leaned back a fraction. "So someone already tried and failed to retrieve it."

"No," said the admiral. "No one has been allowed in yet."

That caught Richard's attention.

The planet image narrowed further until one region stood highlighted—an enormous forest expanse marked by winding rivers, elevated ridges, and a dense canopy that covered nearly everything beneath it.

"The forest is called the Eldergreen Expanse," Admiral Taylor said. "Kael Thorn entered it after the crash carrying the StarPath Core. He later emerged without it."

Milo looked up. "He left it there."

"Yes."

The civilian security officer spoke again.

"A second individual was later apprehended," the civilian officer said. "An associate of Thorn's. He attempted to negotiate a reduced sentence by providing what he claimed was a route back to the device."

The display shifted slightly, refining the map's edges.

"According to his statement, Thorn carried the Core into the preserve. The two of them traveled together for some distance before separating. Thorn continued inward. The associate withdrew and recorded what he could of the route on his way out."

Dooley's eyebrows went up. "He made a map from inside a protected tribal forest and expected that to go well for him?"

"No," Ashton said. "He expected greed to be smarter than consequences."

The admiral touched the table again.

A rough hand-drawn map appeared, suspended above the surface in pale layered lines.

It looked exactly like the work of a frightened man trying to remember enough to save himself later. Curving river. Split stone marker. Tall white tree. Long ridge. A cave marked with an uncertain symbol and two crossed lines near what might have been a basin or clearing. Some details were dense. Others were almost useless.

Richard leaned in.

Even at first glance, the problem was obvious.

The map had landmarks.

But not enough context.

Commander Hale nodded toward it. "Survey comparison suggests parts of the map align with visible topography near the outer preserve. Rivers, ridges, certain rock formations. But much of the interior is concealed by canopy density. Satellite imaging helps only so much."

"Meaning," Ashton said, "the map is half useful and half imagination."

"Not imagination," said the admiral. "Memory under stress."

Richard studied the lines. "How accurate do we think it is?"

The civilian officer answered. "Accurate enough to matter. Incomplete enough to be dangerous."

That felt right.

Milo kept looking at the map, his expression thoughtful. "He drew it while leaving?"

"Yes," said Hale. "From memory, and under pressure."

"So it tells where he noticed things," Milo said, "not necessarily where the safest path is."

Admiral Taylor gave a small nod. "Correct."

Richard sat back slightly. The shape of the problem was clearer now. Protected territory. Stolen device. Unreliable map. A political situation delicate enough that the wrong approach could cause damage far beyond one missing piece of equipment.

But there was still one question sitting in the room.

Why them?

Admiral Taylor seemed to read it before anyone asked.

"The local government has agreed to discuss a retrieval mission," he said. "Not a search operation in force. Not a military incursion. A small, low-impact expedition under strict legal and cultural limits."

Dooley slowly turned his head toward Richard, then Ashton, then Milo, as if confirming they were all hearing the same thing.

The admiral continued.

"The kingdom governing that hemisphere has made it clear that any team allowed entry must be minimal in number, respectful of forest law, adaptable under restriction, and capable of operating without the technological advantages normally relied upon in missions of this type."

Ashton folded her hands on the table. "So no heavy scan package."

"No."

"No autonomous drone sweep."

"No."

"No powered trail breach."

"Absolutely not."

Dooley looked mildly offended on behalf of modern convenience.

Richard asked the question that mattered most. "And if the team violates those terms?"

The room grew just a shade quieter.

"Then," Admiral Taylor said, "the mission ends, diplomatic trust is damaged, and the StarPath Core may remain where it is indefinitely."

No one spoke for a moment after that.

Richard glanced back to the forest image, then to the map, then finally to the admiral.

The answer had not been spoken yet.

But it was already there.

Admiral Taylor rested both hands lightly on the edge of the table.

"I am assigning the four of you to the retrieval team."

Even expecting it, Richard felt the words land with weight.

Dooley blinked hard.

Ashton's eyes narrowed—not in refusal, but in concentration. She always looked a little more intense when she was absorbing something important.

Milo did not move at all, though Richard could see the quickening focus in his face.

The admiral went on.

"You are being assigned because this mission requires a smaller footprint than a standard operations unit would create. It requires judgment, restraint, adaptability, and the ability to function as a team under unusual cultural and environmental constraints. You have demonstrated those qualities often enough that I'm willing to trust them where trust is now required."

That did something quiet to the room.

Richard felt it especially because the admiral had not raised his voice or dressed the statement up with ceremony. He had simply said it. Trust. Required.

Commander Hale touched the table and the display shifted again, this time showing a set of mission parameters arranged in clean columns.

Primary Objective: Recover Quantum StarPath Core
Secondary Objective: Preserve legal and diplomatic standing with Elyndor
Restrictions: No heavy machinery. No invasive scanning. No unauthorized tribal contact. No environmental damage. Non-lethal defense only.

Ashton read through the list once and then asked, "What are we walking into besides trees?"

The civilian officer answered, "Uncertain terrain. Potentially dangerous wildlife. Weather instability in parts of the preserve. And cultural boundaries that must be respected even when inconvenient."

Dooley looked at the forest image again. "That is a very elegant way to say we could get lost, mauled, soaked, and arrested."

Admiral Taylor did not disagree. "Which is why you'll be receiving local support."

He touched the display again.

The image shifted one last time.

A city appeared first, built in pale stone and green terraces beneath high towers and broad skybridges. Beyond it, rising in the distance like a living wall, was the dark sweep of the Eldergreen Expanse.

Then another image overlaid it.

A girl about their age. Seventeen perhaps. Composed. Intelligent eyes. Dark hair drawn neatly back. She stood beside a display of preserved botanical specimens and carved tribal relics, one hand resting lightly near a set of notes. She did not look ornamental. She looked attentive. The kind of person who listened hard and remembered everything.

"This," said Admiral Taylor, "is Princess Lydia of Elyndor."

Dooley sat up straighter. "A princess."

Ashton did not take her eyes off the display. "Why do I get the feeling that's not the important part?"

"Because it isn't," said the admiral.

Another image appeared beside Lydia's.

A woman older than the princess by several years, standing in a training yard with a practice staff in hand. Strong posture. Calm face. Controlled presence. Nothing about her invited foolishness.

"Captain Serana Vale," the admiral said. "Royal guard. Personal protector to Princess Lydia."

Dooley looked from one image to the other. "I am beginning to think this mission is more complicated than the first half suggested."

"The princess," Admiral Taylor said, ignoring the interruption with long practice, "has spent years studying the ecology, tribal customs, and preserved history of the Eldergreen Expanse. She has not entered the forest herself, but the Elyndoran court believes her knowledge may prove essential in interpreting Thorn's map and in avoiding legal or cultural violations."

Richard understood immediately. The map alone would not be enough. The terrain alone would not be enough. They needed someone who understood what kinds of meaning a forest like that could hide beneath ordinary-looking landmarks.

Milo spoke quietly. "She's going with us."

"If her father permits it," said the admiral. "Discussions are underway."

Ashton leaned back again, but this time there was something almost thoughtful in it. "So we're not just retrieving stolen equipment. We're entering someone else's protected history."

Admiral Taylor looked at her. "That is exactly correct."

No one spoke after that.

The forest still turned slowly above the table. The rough map hovered beside it. The image of Lydia remained on one side, Serana on the other, as if the mission itself were already beginning to gather its pieces.

Richard felt two things at once.

The first was the simple weight of assignment. Responsibility. Expectation. The knowledge that something important had just shifted and would not shift back.

The second was something quieter.

Curiosity.

Not careless excitement. Not the kind Dooley sometimes let spill out before his caution caught up. This was steadier than that. The sense that the shape of this mission would matter, and not only because of the stolen Core. Something about it felt older. More careful. As if they were not being sent to conquer a problem, but to pass through one without doing harm.

Admiral Taylor deactivated the map but left the planet image in place.

"You depart tomorrow at 0800 aboard Specter One," he said. "You will travel first to the Elyndoran capital, where you will be formally received by the royal court. Permission to enter the forest has not yet been granted. You are not to assume it will be. Your first task is to listen, understand the constraints, and earn local trust."

He looked directly at all four of them.

"Do not make the mistake of thinking this mission begins at the forest boundary. It begins the moment you land."

Richard nodded once. "Yes, sir."

The others echoed him.

Commander Hale gathered the remaining data packets and slid four slim briefing tablets across the table, one to each cadet.

"Initial mission files," she said. "Read them carefully. Especially the legal section. The Elyndorans are not difficult people, but they are serious about what belongs to them."

Dooley accepted his tablet with both hands as though it might explode if mishandled. "Understood."

The civilian officer gave him a tired look that suggested he was too weary to distinguish sincerity from personality.

Admiral Taylor straightened.

"You are dismissed for now. Report to pre-departure prep at 1900. Bring questions then, not assumptions."

There it was again. Calm. Clear. Final.

Richard stood. The others did the same.

For just a moment, as the chairs slid back and the room began to loosen from briefing formality, Richard looked again at the image of the planet still glowing above the table.

Elyndor.

Green. Silent from orbit. Hiding a stolen machine under miles of ancient forest and whatever else the map had failed to explain.

Beside him, Dooley drew a careful breath.

Then another.

Richard knew that sound.

Dooley was trying not to talk until they were outside.

It lasted almost to the door.

Almost.

"A princess," he whispered as they stepped into the corridor. "We are apparently going on a mission with a princess."

Ashton walked past him. "Your ability to identify the least urgent detail continues to amaze me."

"It is not the least urgent detail. It is simply the one with the most story potential."

Milo glanced down at his briefing tablet. "You heard the part about legal restrictions, right?"

"I heard all of it," Dooley said. "I am capable of hearing more than one important thing."

Ashton gave him a look. "That remains under review."

Richard let them go a few steps ahead before looking back once through the narrow glass inset in the briefing room door.

Inside, Admiral Taylor and Commander Hale were already speaking quietly with the civilian officer, their heads bent over the glowing map.

The mission had begun.

Not at the forest.

Not even at the planet.

Right here.

With trust, responsibility, and a rough hand-drawn trail left behind by a frightened thief who had gone where he never should have gone.

Richard turned and followed the others down the corridor.

Tomorrow they would leave.

And somewhere under the ancient canopy of Elyndor, a stolen StarPath Core waited in darkness.

Chapter 2 — Approach to Elyndor

Specter One did not announce its departure.

It simply moved.

One moment it rested within the quiet structure of the station's outer dock, held in place by clamps and guidance rails, surrounded by the low murmur of systems at idle. The next, those restraints released, and the ship eased forward with a smooth, deliberate motion that barely disturbed the space around it.

Inside, the transition was felt more than seen.

A subtle shift in pressure.

A change in vibration beneath the deck.

The quiet awareness that they were no longer attached to anything but themselves.

Richard Taylor stood near the forward observation panel, one hand resting lightly against the frame as the station began to drift backward in the viewport. He had watched departures before. Many of them. But each time carried its own tone, its own sense of beginning.

This one felt… different.

Not heavier exactly.

But more deliberate.

Behind him, Dooley Lewis leaned slightly to one side, trying to get a better angle past Richard's shoulder without actually asking him to move.

"I always forget how quiet it is," Dooley said.

Ashton Quinn, seated at one of the side consoles with her tablet open, didn't look up. "That's because you usually talk through the part where you're supposed to notice it."

"I am noticing it now."

"You are describing it now."

"That's part of noticing."

Milo Santiago stood a few steps back, his gaze shifting between the retreating station and the planet beyond. He didn't say anything, but his attention lingered longer on the planet. It filled more of the viewport with every passing second, its curved horizon bright against the darkness.

Elyndor.

Even from orbit, it didn't look like most of the inhabited worlds Richard had seen.

There were cities, yes. You could see them along the coasts and in the more open regions—clusters of light and structure that marked civilization clearly enough. But what defined the planet wasn't the cities.

It was everything between them.

Green.

Deep, layered green that spread across entire continents in vast uninterrupted stretches. Forests so large they seemed to shape the geography itself, pushing rivers into long curves and wrapping mountain ranges in living texture.

Richard found himself focusing on one region in particular.

The eastern hemisphere.

Even from this distance, the Eldergreen Expanse stood out. A darker mass within the broader green, denser somehow, as if the canopy there absorbed more light than it reflected.

"Hard to believe something that big is mostly untouched," Dooley said quietly.

Richard nodded. "It's not untouched."

Dooley glanced at him. "You know what I mean."

"Yeah," Richard said. "I do."

Ashton finally looked up from her tablet and followed their line of sight. "Protected doesn't mean empty. It just means the rules are different."

Milo spoke softly. "And probably older."

That felt right too.

Specter One adjusted its orientation, the planet shifting slightly in the viewport as the ship aligned for descent trajectory. The motion was smooth enough that it might have gone unnoticed if not for the slow, steady change in perspective.

"Atmospheric entry in fourteen minutes," came the calm voice of the ship's AI.

Mother.

She did not raise her voice. She did not emphasize. She simply stated.

Richard had noticed that about her the first time he had been assigned to the vessel. Specter One's systems were among the most advanced in their fleet, and yet its AI did not behave like some of the more expressive models used on training ships. There was no attempt at personality, no unnecessary commentary. Just clarity.

"Course stable," Mother continued. "Descent vector confirmed."

Dooley nodded as if the AI could see him. "Good. I like when things are stable."

Ashton closed her tablet and set it aside. "You like when things are predictable."

"That too."

Richard stepped back from the viewport and turned toward the others. "We should review once more before we land."

Ashton was already reaching for her tablet again. "Map first?"

"Map first," Richard agreed.

Milo moved closer, and Dooley followed, though he took a seat rather than standing.

The projection activated between them, rising from the center console in a soft lattice of light. The thief's map appeared again, hovering at an angle that allowed all of them to see.

Even now, after reviewing it multiple times, it still looked the same.

Rough.

Inconsistent.

Just detailed enough to be useful.

Just incomplete enough to be dangerous.

Ashton pointed to a section near the outer edge. "This part aligns with satellite imagery. River bend, ridge line, that cluster of rock formations. We should be able to confirm our starting position once we enter."

Milo leaned in slightly. "After that, it gets less certain."

"Much less," Ashton said. "These interior markers…" She tapped lightly near one of the symbols. "There's no way to know how many 'white trees' he saw or how far apart they actually are."

Dooley frowned. "We're really going to be following something that says 'big tree, then maybe another big tree'?"

"That is a simplified version," Ashton said.

"It is also accurate."

Richard studied the map in silence for a moment.

"What about elevation?" he asked.

Ashton shifted the overlay. "Limited data. Canopy density blocks most surface detail. We'll get general terrain—hills, cliffs, major formations—but nothing precise once we're under the trees."

"So we confirm what we can early," Richard said, thinking it through aloud, "and after that we rely on pattern and consistency."

"And Lydia," Dooley added.

Ashton gave a small nod. "Mostly Lydia."

Milo's eyes remained on the map. "He drew it while leaving."

Richard glanced at him. "Yeah."

"So everything here," Milo said, "is what stood out to him on the way out. Not necessarily what mattered on the way in."

Ashton looked at him, then back at the projection. "That would explain the imbalance."

"Meaning?" Dooley asked.

"It means," Ashton said, "that some of the most important things might not be on the map at all."

That settled quietly over them.

Richard let it sit for a moment before nodding. "Then we don't treat the map like instructions."

"We treat it like clues," Milo said.

"Exactly."

Dooley leaned back slightly. "I am beginning to understand why this was not assigned to a larger team."

Ashton smirked faintly. "Because a larger team would get lost more efficiently."

"That is not comforting."

"It's accurate."

Mother's voice returned.

"Ten minutes to atmospheric entry."

Richard deactivated the projection.

"Alright," he said. "Once we land, we listen first. No assumptions."

Dooley raised a hand slightly. "That was also in the briefing."

"Good," Richard said. "Then we remember it."

Ashton stood, stretching one arm across her back. "And we try not to offend an entire planetary government on the first day."

"Also good," Richard said.

Milo glanced once more toward the viewport.

The planet was close now.

Very close.

Cloud formations drifted slowly across the upper atmosphere, their edges catching the light of the system's star. Through gaps in the cloud cover, the surface showed in greater detail—rivers threading through dense forest, mountain ridges casting long shadows, and, in one region, the unmistakable edge where structured land gave way to something older.

The Eldergreen Expanse.

Even from above, it did not look like a place that welcomed intrusion.

Specter One tilted slightly as it entered the upper atmosphere. The first faint tremor ran through the hull, subtle but unmistakable. A soft glow formed along the edges of the forward viewport as heat built across the outer plating.

Dooley shifted in his seat. "There it is."

"Normal," Ashton said.

"I know it's normal. I'm just acknowledging it."

Richard returned to the observation panel, watching as the stars faded and the sky shifted from black to deep blue. The transition always came quickly, but it never felt rushed. More like stepping from one world into another without passing through anything in between.

Clouds enveloped the ship briefly, turning the outside view into a shifting field of white and gray. Then they broke through.

The city appeared.

Not all at once.

First the outer edges—structured fields, terraced land, roadways that curved with the natural shape of the terrain rather than cutting across it. Then the central rise, where the main city stood.

Elyndor's capital did not resemble the dense vertical towers of some off-world colonies. It rose more gradually, built in layers that followed the land's contours. Pale stone and living greenery blended together, buildings connected by open walkways and high bridges that allowed air and light to move freely between them.

It looked… balanced.

Intentional.

As if someone had taken care not to disturb what had been there before.

"Okay," Dooley said quietly. "That's impressive."

Ashton nodded once. "Efficient use of terrain."

"That is not what I meant."

"I know."

Milo's gaze shifted beyond the city, toward the distant horizon.

Even from here, he could see it.

A darker line.

Not sharp.

Not defined.

But present.

The forest.

Richard followed his gaze.

There was something about it that drew the eye even from a distance. Not because it stood out in color, but because of how it seemed to hold itself. The land around it felt open, structured, understood.

That region did not.

"That's where we're going," Dooley said.

No one answered.

They didn't need to.

Mother's voice broke the silence.

"Landing approach confirmed. Elyndor capital clearance granted. Royal escort inbound."

Richard straightened slightly. "That was fast."

Ashton glanced at her tablet. "They knew we were coming."

"Still," Dooley said, "escort sounds official."

"It is official," Ashton said.

"More official than I expected."

Richard didn't respond. His attention had shifted forward again.

Two smaller craft were rising from the city below, their shapes sleek and symmetrical, moving with controlled precision as they angled upward to meet Specter One's descent path. They positioned themselves on either side of the ship, maintaining perfect distance without appearing aggressive.

An escort.

Not a warning.

But not casual either.

Milo watched them closely. "They're matching our speed exactly."

"Of course they are," Ashton said. "They're very good at this."

Dooley leaned slightly toward the viewport. "Do we wave?"

"No," Ashton said.

"Just asking."

Richard felt the subtle change in the ship's motion as Specter One adjusted to align with the escort's guidance. The city grew larger beneath them, details sharpening—individual structures, open courtyards, lines of people moving along elevated walkways.

"Final descent," Mother said.

The ship lowered smoothly, passing over the outer terraces and into a designated landing zone set slightly apart from the main flow of the city. The platform was wide, open, and clearly prepared for arrivals of this kind.

The engines softened.

The motion slowed.

Then stopped.

For a moment, nothing happened.

The kind of stillness that comes at the end of a long movement.

Dooley let out a slow breath. "We're here."

Richard nodded once.

"Yeah," he said quietly. "We are."

Outside, the escort craft settled into position nearby.

And somewhere beyond the edges of the city, unseen but waiting, the Eldergreen Expanse stretched across the horizon.

Ancient.

Protected.

And holding something they had come a very long way to find.

Chapter 3 — The Royal Audience

The landing platform remained quiet for several seconds after the engines powered down.

Not silent.

Never silent.

There were always sounds—air currents shifting across open space, distant movement from nearby structures, the soft settling of a ship that had just completed descent. But compared to the motion and vibration of travel, the stillness felt deliberate, almost expectant.

Richard Taylor stood near the forward hatch as it cycled through its final checks. Behind him, the others gathered without speaking, each of them watching the status indicators more closely than they needed to.

It wasn't nerves.

Not exactly.

It was awareness.

They were no longer operating in familiar space.

"External atmosphere stable," Mother said calmly. "No environmental concerns detected. Awaiting clearance to open."

Richard glanced once toward Ashton.

She gave a small nod. "Everything matches what we were given."

Dooley shifted his weight slightly. "So this is the part where we step out and try not to embarrass ourselves immediately."

"That is always the part," Ashton said.

Milo said nothing, but his gaze moved toward the hatch as if he were trying to see through it.

A soft tone sounded.

"Clearance granted," Mother said.

The hatch began to open.

Light spilled inward first.

Not harsh, not blinding—just clean, natural light that carried with it a subtle warmth. Air followed a moment later, fresh and faintly scented with something Richard couldn't immediately place. Not artificial. Not processed. Something… living.

The ramp lowered smoothly.

For a moment, none of them moved.

Then Richard stepped forward.

Outside, the landing platform stretched wide and open, its surface formed from pale stone that reflected the daylight without glare. The escort craft that had guided them down now rested at opposite edges of the platform, their engines quiet, their presence steady but unobtrusive.

And waiting at the base of the ramp—

Were people.

Not a crowd.

Not a spectacle.

A small, composed delegation.

Richard took in the details as he descended.

Three uniformed guards stood slightly apart, their posture upright but not rigid. Their attire was not identical to anything he had seen in UESC service—lighter, more flexible, designed for movement rather than display. No visible heavy weapons. Only compact, restrained equipment positioned where it could be reached quickly if needed.

Between them stood a single man in formal attire, his clothing marked by subtle patterns rather than insignia. His hands were folded calmly in front of him, his expression attentive rather than guarded.

And beside him—

She stood slightly behind and to the right.

Not in hiding.

Not in shadow.

But not positioned as the center either.

Princess Lydia.

Richard knew it before the man spoke, before any introduction was made. There was something in the way she carried herself—aware of her surroundings, attentive to the moment, but not demanding it. She observed first.

That alone set her apart.

Her gaze moved across the group as they approached, not quickly, not superficially. She noticed things. Posture. Movement. The way they walked down the ramp. Richard could tell she was forming impressions, quietly and without announcing them.

He respected that immediately.

The man in formal attire stepped forward as the cadets reached the base of the ramp.

"Welcome to Elyndor," he said, his voice calm and measured. "I am Minister Halvern, representing the royal court."

Richard inclined his head slightly. "Cadet Richard Taylor, United Earth Space Command."

The others introduced themselves in turn.

Ashton, precise and direct.

Dooley, just formal enough to remain appropriate.

Milo, quiet but clear.

The minister acknowledged each of them with equal attention.

"You are expected," Halvern said. "The court has been informed of your arrival and of the purpose of your visit."

He paused briefly, then turned slightly.

"Princess Lydia."

Now she stepped forward.

Not dramatically.

Not with ceremony.

Simply into the space where she could be seen clearly.

Up close, Richard noticed what the image in the briefing had not fully conveyed.

She was young.

Seventeen, perhaps.

But there was nothing uncertain in her presence.

Her expression was composed, but not distant. Curious, but controlled. Her eyes moved from one cadet to another, not lingering too long on any one of them, but not rushing either.

"I am pleased to meet you," she said.

Her voice was steady, clear, and carried easily without effort.

"Welcome to Elyndor."

Dooley opened his mouth.

Closed it.

Then nodded.

"Thank you," he said, managing to keep his tone respectful.

Ashton gave a small, precise nod.

Milo inclined his head slightly.

Richard met her gaze briefly. "It's an honor."

Lydia acknowledged the words, but her attention had already shifted slightly—past them, toward the ship.

"Your vessel," she said, almost to herself. "It is… different from those we typically receive."

Ashton followed her gaze. "It's designed for low-profile operations."

Lydia nodded once. "I thought as much."

There was no judgment in her tone.

Only observation.

Another presence stepped forward then.

From the side.

Not announced.

Not introduced.

But immediately understood.

Captain Serana Vale.

She moved with a quiet precision that drew attention without asking for it. Taller than Lydia, her posture perfectly balanced, her eyes scanning not just the cadets but the space around them. The platform. The guards. The ship. Every angle where something could shift unexpectedly.

She stopped just behind Lydia's right shoulder.

Close enough to act.

Far enough to allow.

Richard recognized the role instantly.

Protection.

But not control.

Serana's gaze met his for a brief moment.

Measured.

Evaluating.

Then it moved on.

Satisfied, for now.

Minister Halvern gestured lightly toward the far side of the platform, where a transport awaited.

"The court is prepared to receive you," he said. "If you will follow me."

Richard nodded. "Of course."

They began to move.

The transition from landing platform to city was seamless.

Walkways extended outward from the platform, blending into the architecture in a way that made it difficult to tell where one ended and the other began. The materials shifted subtly underfoot—stone to polished surface to living integration where plant life was not removed but guided.

Dooley leaned slightly toward Ashton as they walked.

"This place doesn't feel built," he said quietly. "It feels… arranged."

Ashton glanced around. "Integrated."

"That's the word."

Milo's attention moved upward.

Bridges crossed overhead, connecting structures at different heights, allowing movement without congestion. People moved along them calmly, without urgency, their pace steady and unforced.

No one rushed.

No one pushed.

It was a different rhythm.

Richard noticed that more than anything.

The absence of hurry.

Lydia walked beside them now, not ahead, not behind.

With them.

"This is your first visit to Elyndor," she said.

It wasn't a question.

"No," Richard said. "It is."

She nodded slightly. "It is often quieter than visitors expect."

Dooley smiled faintly. "Quiet is good."

"Sometimes," Lydia said.

There was something in that answer.

Not disagreement.

But experience.

They reached the transport—a long, open-sided vehicle designed to move smoothly through the city without enclosing its passengers completely. As they took their places, Richard noticed that the seating arrangement was not accidental.

Lydia sat where she could see both the cadets and the path ahead.

Serana positioned herself where she could see everything.

Minister Halvern remained forward, guiding but not dominating.

The transport began to move.

The city unfolded around them.

Terraced gardens.

Open courtyards.

Structures that rose not in sharp lines but in curves that followed the land.

And always, beyond it all—

The horizon.

The line of the forest.

Even from here, it was visible.

Distant.

Waiting.

Lydia followed Richard's gaze.

"The Eldergreen Expanse," she said quietly.

He nodded.

"You've studied it."

"Yes."

She did not elaborate immediately.

Instead, she watched the horizon for a moment longer.

"From maps," she said at last. "From records. From accounts passed down over generations."

Her tone shifted slightly.

Not uncertain.

But reflective.

"I have not seen it from within."

That mattered.

Richard understood that at once.

"You're going with us," Dooley said, unable to keep the question out of his voice.

Lydia glanced at him.

"Perhaps," she said.

"That decision has not yet been made."

Ashton looked at her. "You want to."

It wasn't a challenge.

Just a statement.

Lydia met her gaze.

"Yes."

Again, no hesitation.

No embellishment.

Just truth.

Serana's voice came quietly from behind.

"If permission is granted," she said, "it will not be without conditions."

Dooley nodded slowly. "That seems… fair."

The transport continued forward.

The city began to rise slightly as they approached the central district, where the structures grew more formal, more defined. The openness remained, but there was a sense of purpose here that had not been as present in the outer terraces.

Ahead, the royal complex came into view.

Not a palace in the traditional sense.

Not towering.

Not imposing.

But unmistakable.

A place of decision.

Of history.

Of responsibility.

As the transport slowed, Richard felt the shift again.

The same one he had felt in the briefing room.

The quiet recognition that the next step mattered.

Lydia rose as the vehicle came to a stop.

Serana stepped with her.

Minister Halvern turned back toward the cadets.

"The King and Queen will receive you now," he said.

No one spoke.

They stepped down from the transport together.

And moved forward.

Toward the place where permission would either be given—

Or denied.

And somewhere beyond that decision—

The forest waited.

Chapter 4 — The Weight of Permission

The entrance to the royal complex was open.

Not unguarded.

But open.

There were no massive gates, no towering barriers meant to impress or intimidate. Instead, the approach widened into a broad stone pathway that led directly into the heart of the structure. The guards stationed along its edges stood quietly at attention, their presence unmistakable but not aggressive.

They were not there to keep people out.

They were there to ensure that those who entered understood where they were.

Richard noticed that immediately.

The group moved forward together, their footsteps soft against the smooth stone. The air felt different here—still natural, still carrying the faint scent of growing things—but with a deeper calm, as though the space itself had been shaped to encourage careful thought.

Inside, the architecture opened upward.

Light filtered down from above through wide, angled panels that allowed the sky to remain visible even within the structure. Walls curved rather than met sharply, guiding movement rather than directing it. Water flowed somewhere nearby—not loud, not distracting, but present in a steady, gentle rhythm.

Dooley leaned slightly toward Ashton as they walked.

"I feel like if I say something too loud, the building will notice."

Ashton kept her voice low. "Then don't test that theory."

"I wasn't planning to. I'm just… acknowledging it."

Milo said nothing, but his eyes moved constantly, taking in the layout, the spacing, the subtle ways the structure seemed to direct attention without forcing it.

Serana walked just behind Lydia now, her posture unchanged, her awareness constant. But Richard noticed something else as well.

She was not tense.

Alert, yes.

Prepared, always.

But not tense.

That said something about this place.

Minister Halvern led them through a series of open corridors that gradually narrowed—not in a restrictive way, but in a way that focused direction. The wider public spaces gave way to more formal passageways, the sounds of the outer complex fading until only their own movement and the distant flow of water remained.

At the end of the final corridor, the space opened again.

The audience chamber.

It was not large in the way Richard had expected.

It did not need to be.

The room held its presence through proportion, not size. The ceiling rose high enough to draw the eye upward, where light entered in soft, angled beams. The floor was smooth and unbroken, leading naturally toward the far end of the chamber where two figures stood.

Not seated.

Standing.

Waiting.

King Gregory and Queen Josephine.

They did not stand on a raised platform.

They did not separate themselves from the room.

They stood on the same level as those who entered, positioned where they could be seen clearly, but not elevated beyond reach.

Richard felt something settle into place in his understanding at that moment.

This was not a kingdom built on distance.

It was built on presence.

Minister Halvern stepped forward and inclined his head.

"Your Majesties," he said, "the cadets have arrived."

The King nodded once.

"Thank you, Halvern."

His voice was calm, measured, and carried easily through the chamber without force.

"Leave us."

The minister bowed slightly and stepped aside, moving quietly out of the room. The guards remained at a respectful distance near the entrance, unobtrusive but attentive.

Silence followed.

Not uncomfortable.

But intentional.

King Gregory stepped forward.

He was older than Richard had expected—not frail, not diminished, but marked by time in ways that spoke of long responsibility rather than decline. His expression was open, his eyes attentive, and there was something in the way he moved that suggested patience more than authority.

Queen Josephine stood beside him.

Where the King felt warm and steady, the Queen's presence was sharper. Not harsh. Not unkind. But precise. Her gaze moved across the cadets with careful attention, taking in details that Richard suspected very few people ever noticed about themselves.

Together, they formed a balance.

Richard stepped forward slightly.

"Your Majesties," he said. "Cadet Richard Taylor, United Earth Space Command."

The others followed in turn.

Ashton, composed and direct.

Dooley, careful and respectful.

Milo, quiet but steady.

The King acknowledged each of them with equal attention.

"You are welcome here," he said. "Though I understand your purpose is not one that allows for a long visit."

There was no accusation in the words.

Only recognition.

Richard nodded. "We appreciate the audience."

The King's gaze shifted briefly toward Lydia.

She stood slightly to one side, not hidden, but not centered. Observing.

Learning.

Queen Josephine spoke then.

"We have been informed of the situation," she said. "A stolen device. A crash. A forest that was not meant to be entered."

Her eyes returned to the cadets.

"You understand where that leaves us."

It was not a question.

Richard answered anyway.

"Yes, ma'am."

The King clasped his hands lightly in front of him.

"The Eldergreen Expanse is not simply land under our authority," he said. "It is a trust. One that has been held for generations before us, and one we intend to preserve for those who will come after."

He paused, allowing the words to settle.

"No one enters lightly," he continued. "Not even those who rule here."

That was not a statement of pride.

It was a statement of responsibility.

Ashton spoke carefully. "We were told that entry requires permission."

"It does," the Queen said. "And not easily given."

Dooley shifted slightly, but did not speak.

Milo's gaze remained steady, focused on the King.

Richard felt the weight of the moment clearly now.

This was the decision point.

Not the forest.

Not the mission.

This.

The King looked at them for a long moment before continuing.

"The device you seek," he said, "does not belong to this world. But where it rests now does."

That was the line.

Clear.

Uncompromising.

Richard nodded once. "We understand."

The Queen studied him briefly, then spoke again.

"Do you?" she asked.

There was no challenge in her tone.

Only expectation.

Richard held her gaze.

"We understand that retrieving it cannot come at the cost of what is already there."

The room remained still for a moment.

Then the King inclined his head slightly.

"That is a beginning," he said.

Lydia stepped forward then.

Not abruptly.

Not intrusively.

But with purpose.

"Father," she said.

The word was simple.

But it carried weight.

The King turned toward her.

"Yes, Lydia."

She met his gaze, then glanced briefly toward the cadets.

"The map they carry," she said, "will not be enough."

The Queen's eyes shifted to her.

"Explain."

Lydia stepped fully into the space now, her posture steady.

"The landmarks described are incomplete," she said. "Some are distinctive. Others are not. Without context, they could be misread. Paths could be chosen incorrectly. Tribal boundaries could be crossed without intent."

She paused.

"And the forest does not forgive that easily."

Serana remained still behind her.

But her attention sharpened.

The King considered his daughter's words carefully.

"You believe you can provide that context," he said.

"Yes."

No hesitation.

No uncertainty.

The Queen's gaze narrowed slightly—not in disapproval, but in evaluation.

"You have studied the forest," she said. "You have not walked it."

"That is true," Lydia said.

"And yet you would enter it."

"Yes."

Again, simple.

Direct.

Honest.

The room held that for a moment.

The King looked at her for a long time.

Not as a ruler.

As a father.

"There are risks you cannot fully understand," he said quietly.

Lydia nodded.

"I know."

"You do not," he said.

Her expression did not change.

"No," she said. "Not completely."

That mattered.

Richard saw it.

So did the Queen.

Lydia continued.

"But I understand enough to know that they will need guidance," she said. "And I am the one best prepared to give it."

Serana's voice came quietly.

"If she goes, I go."

It was not offered as a condition.

It was simply fact.

The Queen looked at Serana, then back to Lydia.

"You would leave the safety of this place," she said, "to walk into a region even our rangers do not enter freely."

"Yes."

The King exhaled slowly.

Not frustration.

Not reluctance.

Weight.

Responsibility.

The same thing Lydia had begun to understand.

He turned back toward the cadets.

"If permission is granted," he said, "it will not be without conditions."

Richard nodded. "We expected that."

The Queen stepped forward slightly.

"You will not enter as explorers," she said. "You will not enter as claimants. You will enter as guests under restriction."

Her gaze moved across each of them.

"You will follow the laws of the forest. You will respect the territories of its people. You will not take what does not belong to you. And you will leave no mark that cannot be undone."

Each word was clear.

Measured.

Final.

Dooley swallowed slightly, then nodded.

"Yes, ma'am."

Ashton inclined her head.

"Understood."

Milo said quietly, "We will."

Richard met the Queen's gaze.

"We agree."

The King looked once more to Lydia.

Then to Serana.

Then back to the cadets.

The silence stretched just long enough to be felt.

Then—

"We will consider your request," he said.

Not a yes.

Not a no.

But something more important.

A decision in motion.

The Queen turned slightly.

"You will be given time to rest," she said. "And to review what you believe you know."

Her eyes returned to Lydia.

"And to decide what you are willing to carry."

That was not directed only at the cadets.

Lydia understood that.

Richard could see it.

Minister Halvern reappeared at the entrance.

The King inclined his head.

"For now," he said, "you are our guests."

The audience was over.

Not concluded.

Not resolved.

But begun.

As they turned to leave, Richard felt the shift again.

The mission had changed.

It was no longer about reaching the forest.

It was about being allowed to enter it.

And that—

Would not be given lightly.

Chapter 5 — The Quiet Before Decision

The guest quarters were set apart from the main flow of the royal complex.

Not isolated.

But quieter.

The corridors leading there were narrower, the lighting softer, the sounds of the larger structure fading into something more distant and indistinct. It felt less like a place for receiving visitors and more like a place for allowing them to settle.

To think.

To consider.

Richard Taylor paused just inside the doorway as the others stepped in behind him. The room itself was simple, but carefully arranged. Four sleeping alcoves curved along one wall, each separated just enough to give a sense of privacy without closing anyone off entirely. A central table stood beneath a wide window that opened outward toward the terraces beyond, where greenery climbed in layered patterns between stonework and open air.

Dooley stepped in fully and turned slowly in place.

"This is…" he began, then stopped.

Ashton set her tablet on the table. "Comfortable."

"I was going to say unexpectedly comfortable."

"That too."

Milo moved toward the window. He rested his hand lightly against the frame and looked out over the city. From this height, the terraces flowed outward in gentle steps, leading the eye toward the distant horizon where the forest line rested like a quiet boundary between two different worlds.

He didn't say anything.

He didn't need to.

Richard set his own tablet down beside Ashton's and exhaled slowly. The movement was subtle, but it marked a shift. The briefing was behind them. The audience with the King and Queen had been… something more than formal.

Now there was time.

Not much.

But enough.

"Alright," Richard said. "Let's go over what we know."

Dooley dropped into one of the chairs. "We know we are waiting."

"That's part of it."

"We also know the forest is very serious about itself."

"That too."

Ashton leaned slightly against the edge of the table. "We know the map is incomplete."

Milo glanced back from the window. "And that we won't get a second chance if we get it wrong."

That settled the tone.

Richard nodded. "So we don't get it wrong."

Dooley gave him a look. "That is a bold strategy."

"It's the only one we have."

A soft knock sounded at the door.

All four of them turned.

Richard moved to open it.

Princess Lydia stood on the other side.

Serana Vale just behind her.

Not blocking the doorway.

But not far from it either.

"May we come in?" Lydia asked.

Her tone was polite, but direct.

Richard stepped aside immediately. "Of course."

She entered without hesitation, her gaze moving briefly across the room before settling on the table where the tablets rested. Serana followed, taking a position near the wall where she could see both the room and the corridor beyond.

Always positioned.

Always aware.

Lydia approached the table slowly.

"You have been reviewing the map," she said.

It wasn't a question.

Ashton nodded. "Trying to."

Lydia reached out and activated the projection.

The rough lines of Kael Thorn's map rose again into the air between them.

Even here, in the calm of the guest quarters, it looked uncertain.

Incomplete.

Lydia studied it for a long moment before speaking.

"The one who drew this was afraid," she said quietly

Dooley blinked. "You can tell that from this?"

"Yes."

She traced one of the lines lightly.

"These marks are not consistent. Here—" she indicated a section where the path shifted abruptly, "—he changed direction without clear reason. That is not planned movement. That is reaction."

Milo stepped closer. "To something he saw?"

"Or thought he saw."

Lydia looked up.

"The forest does that."

There was no dramatics in the way she said it.

Just fact.

Ashton folded her arms slightly. "Meaning?"

"Meaning it overwhelms people who are not prepared for it," Lydia said. "Sound carries differently. Light shifts under the canopy. Movement at the edges of vision is not always what it seems."

She paused.

"And when fear begins to guide your decisions, you stop observing clearly."

Dooley nodded slowly. "That sounds… familiar."

Ashton glanced at him. "From what experience?"

"From being chased by instructors during drills."

"That is not the same."

"It feels the same."

Lydia allowed the faintest hint of a smile.

Then it faded.

"He marked what stood out to him," she continued. "Not what mattered."

Richard nodded. "We were thinking the same."

Lydia looked at him briefly.

"Good."

She shifted the projection slightly, aligning it with a broader topographic overlay from their tablets.

"Some of these markers will help," she said. "The river bend. The ridge line. The stone formation here—" she tapped a point on the map, "—that one is distinctive enough to identify."

"And the rest?" Ashton asked.

Lydia met her gaze.

"The rest will require interpretation."

Serana spoke for the first time.

"And restraint."

The room quieted slightly.

Richard looked toward her.

"Meaning?"

Serana's eyes moved briefly to the map, then back to him.

"You will see paths that look easier," she said. "Clearings that seem safe. Routes that appear direct."

She paused.

"They may not be."

Milo nodded slightly. "Because of tribal territory."

"Yes," Lydia said. "And because of the forest itself."

Dooley leaned forward. "How do we tell the difference?"

Lydia didn't answer immediately.

Instead, she deactivated the projection.

The room dimmed slightly as the light faded.

"You don't," she said.

That got their full attention.

"You learn to recognize when you don't know enough," she continued. "And you stop."

That was not the answer Dooley had hoped for.

"I was hoping for something more… decisive."

Lydia met his gaze.

"That is the decisive part."

Silence followed.

Richard felt something shift again.

Not in the room.

In his understanding.

This wasn't going to be a mission where they solved problems by pushing forward.

It was going to be one where they survived by knowing when not to.

Ashton nodded slowly. "That's going to slow us down."

"Yes," Lydia said.

"And if we don't?"

Lydia's expression didn't change.

"Then the forest will slow you down instead."

That answered that.

Milo returned his gaze to the window.

The forest line was still there.

Distant.

Unmoving.

Waiting.

"Why does your father protect it so strictly?" he asked quietly.

Lydia followed his gaze.

"For the same reason you do not take something that belongs to someone else," she said.

Dooley shifted slightly. "Because it's wrong."

"Yes."

She looked back at them.

"And because the damage lasts longer than the moment."

That landed deeper.

Richard saw it in the way Ashton's posture shifted slightly, in the way Milo's expression tightened just a fraction.

Even Dooley didn't respond right away.

Lydia continued.

"The tribes within the forest have lived there longer than our kingdom has existed in its current form," she said. "Their boundaries are not lines on a map. They are part of how they live. How they understand the world."

She paused.

"If we cross those boundaries without understanding them, we do not just risk ourselves."

"We risk them," Milo said.

"Yes."

Serana's voice followed quietly.

"And that is not a mistake that can be undone easily."

The room settled into stillness again.

Richard looked at Lydia.

"You've studied all of this," he said.

"Yes."

"But you haven't been inside."

"No."

There was no defensiveness in the answer.

Just truth.

Richard nodded once.

"That matters."

Lydia met his gaze.

"I know."

There it was.

Not uncertainty.

Awareness.

Dooley leaned back slightly. "So we're all doing something new."

Ashton glanced at him. "Some more than others."

"Still counts."

Serana shifted her position slightly, her attention moving briefly toward the door, then back to Lydia.

"You should not stay long," she said quietly.

Lydia nodded.

"One more moment."

She turned back to the cadets.

"If permission is granted," she said, "we will not have the luxury of extended planning once we enter."

She looked at each of them in turn.

"You will need to trust what I tell you," she said.

"And I will need to trust that you will act carefully."

Richard answered first.

"We will."

Ashton nodded. "Agreed."

Milo said quietly, "Yes."

Dooley raised a hand slightly. "Also yes."

Lydia held their gaze for a moment longer.

Then inclined her head slightly.

"Then we will be ready."

She turned toward the door.

Serana moved with her.

Before stepping out, Lydia paused.

Just briefly.

Without turning fully back.

"When the decision is made," she said, "it will not be because we convinced them."

She glanced over her shoulder.

"It will be because they believe we understand what we are asking."

Then she stepped into the corridor.

Serana followed.

The door closed softly behind them.

For a moment, none of the cadets spoke.

Then Dooley exhaled.

"Well," he said quietly, "that felt important."

Ashton nodded. "It was."

Milo remained at the window.

Watching the horizon.

Richard looked down at the table where the map had been.

Then back toward the door.

The decision hadn't been made yet.

But something else had.

They were no longer just preparing to enter a forest.

They were preparing to be allowed into it.

And that—

Was going to matter more than anything else that followed.

Chapter 6 — Permission Granted

The message came sooner than Richard expected.

But not quickly enough to feel easy.

It arrived without ceremony—no announcement, no formal escort at first. Just a soft tone at the door and a quiet voice from the corridor requesting their presence.

Richard stood immediately.

The others followed without question.

No one spoke as they stepped out into the hall.

The air felt different.

Not changed in any physical way, but shaped by what they all understood without saying.

The decision had been made.

They walked the same path as before, through the gently curving corridors of the royal complex, past the filtered light and the quiet presence of water somewhere just out of sight. But this time, the space felt more focused.

More final.

Minister Halvern met them halfway.

"The King and Queen will receive you again," he said. "Please follow."

His tone was the same as before.

Calm.

Measured.

But there was no need now for explanation.

Richard nodded once. "Of course."

They continued forward.

This time, Lydia and Serana were not with them.

Richard noticed that immediately.

And understood.

Whatever decision had been made, it had been made first with her.

The audience chamber opened ahead.

As before, the King and Queen stood waiting.

As before, they stood on the same level.

But something in the room had shifted.

Not tension.

Not formality.

Weight.

The kind that settles in after a choice has been carefully considered and cannot be undone.

Richard stepped forward.

"Your Majesties."

The others followed.

The King inclined his head slightly.

"Cadets."

The Queen's gaze moved across them, steady and clear.

"You have been patient," she said.

"We appreciate the consideration," Richard replied.

The King clasped his hands lightly.

"We have reviewed your request," he said. "We have considered the necessity of retrieving the device, the potential consequences of leaving it where it is, and the risks associated with allowing entry into the Eldergreen Expanse."

He paused.

Not for effect.

But to ensure nothing was rushed.

Then—

"Permission will be granted."

The words settled into the room.

Not loudly.

But with certainty.

Dooley inhaled slightly, then caught himself.

Ashton remained still, but her focus sharpened.

Milo did not move at all.

Richard nodded once.

"Thank you, sir."

The King's expression did not change.

"Do not thank me yet," he said gently.

The Queen stepped forward slightly.

"This permission is conditional," she said. "And those conditions are not suggestions."

Richard straightened slightly. "We understand."

"You will," the Queen said, "enter as a limited expedition under royal authority. You will carry no heavy equipment, no invasive scanning devices, and no tools that alter the environment beyond immediate necessity."

Her gaze moved across each of them.

"You will not cross into tribal territory unless invited. You will not attempt communication unless it is initiated. You will not collect artifacts from any site that bears cultural or spiritual significance."

Dooley nodded carefully.

"Yes, ma'am."

Ashton inclined her head. "Understood."

Milo said quietly, "We will follow those terms."

Richard held her gaze. "We agree."

The Queen studied them for a moment longer.

Then nodded once.

The King spoke again.

"You will not enter alone."

Richard expected that.

"Princess Lydia will accompany you."

There it was.

The shift from possibility to reality.

Richard glanced briefly toward the side entrance.

As if on cue—

It opened.

Lydia stepped into the chamber.

Serana at her side.

But this was not the same Lydia who had stood quietly observing before.

There was something different now.

Not outward.

Not dramatic.

But settled.

Resolved.

She moved forward with calm purpose, stopping just short of the King and Queen.

Her gaze met her father's.

Then her mother's.

No words passed between them.

None were needed.

The Queen spoke.

"You understand what this requires."

"Yes," Lydia said.

"You understand that knowledge alone will not protect you."

"Yes."

"You understand that once you enter, you may face decisions that cannot be undone."

A brief pause.

Then—

"Yes."

The King watched her for a long moment.

Not as a ruler.

As a father.

Richard could see it clearly now.

The weight Lydia had spoken of.

The one she had only begun to understand.

"You have studied the forest your entire life," he said quietly.

"Yes."

"You have wanted to see it."

"Yes."

"And now you will."

He paused.

"But not as a student."

Lydia did not look away.

"I know."

The King's expression softened, just slightly.

"Then go as one who understands that what you walk into does not belong to you."

"I will."

Serana stepped forward.

"I will remain at her side," she said.

The Queen nodded once. "You always have."

Serana inclined her head slightly.

The King turned back to the cadets.

"You will follow her guidance in all matters concerning the forest," he said. "Not because she is royalty, but because she understands what you do not."

Richard answered immediately.

"Yes, sir."

Ashton nodded. "Agreed."

Milo said quietly, "We will."

Dooley added, "Absolutely."

The Queen's gaze rested on them a moment longer.

Then she stepped back.

"It is decided."

That was it.

No ceremony.

No proclamation.

Just a decision.

Final.

Minister Halvern stepped forward from the edge of the chamber.

"Preparations will begin immediately," he said. "You will depart at first light."

Richard nodded. "Understood."

The King looked once more at Lydia.

Then at the cadets.

"Rest while you can," he said. "The forest does not measure time as you do."

The meaning was clear.

Once they entered—

Everything would change.

The audience was over.

But as the cadets turned to leave, Richard hesitated just slightly.

He glanced back.

The King and Queen remained where they stood.

Lydia beside them.

Serana just behind.

For a moment, the room held all of it together.

Responsibility.

Trust.

Risk.

Then the moment passed.

Richard turned and followed the others out.

The corridors felt different now.

Not quieter.

Not louder.

Just… clearer.

Dooley exhaled as they rounded the first turn.

"Well," he said softly, "that's real now."

Ashton nodded. "Very."

Milo glanced back briefly toward the chamber, then forward again.

Richard walked in silence for several steps.

Then spoke.

"We move carefully," he said.

"No shortcuts."

"No assumptions."

Ashton gave a small nod. "No mistakes."

Dooley looked at him. "That last one still feels ambitious."

Richard met his gaze.

"Then we make fewer."

That was the best they could do.

Ahead of them, the corridor opened toward the outer terraces.

Beyond that—

The horizon.

And somewhere far beyond that—

The Eldergreen Expanse waited.

And now—

They were going in.

Chapter 7 — The Edge of Entry

Morning came quietly.

There was no alarm.

No sudden shift in the rhythm of the place.

Light simply returned.

Soft at first, filtering through the high panels and open terraces beyond the guest quarters, touching the edges of the room before spreading fully across the floor. The city did not wake all at once. It eased into motion, the sounds of distant movement rising gradually, like something long practiced and never hurried.

Richard Taylor was already awake.

He stood near the window, one hand resting lightly against the frame, watching as the first groups of people began moving along the upper walkways. The same steady pace. The same quiet purpose. Nothing rushed. Nothing wasted.

It was different from the station.

Different from most places he had trained.

He found himself matching that rhythm without thinking about it.

Behind him, Dooley shifted in his alcove and sat up slowly.

"Is it morning," he asked, "or did I just decide it was morning?"

"It's morning," Richard said.

"Good. I prefer when the universe agrees with me."

Ashton was already awake as well, seated at the central table with her tablet open, reviewing the mission parameters again. She didn't look up.

"We depart in less than an hour," she said. "If you plan to have a full conversation with the sunrise, you may want to shorten it."

"I wasn't having a conversation," Dooley said. "I was observing."

"You narrate your observations."

"It helps."

Milo sat up more quietly, his attention already moving toward the window. He didn't speak, but his eyes followed the same distant line they had settled on the day before.

The forest.

Even from here, it was visible.

Not close.

Not immediate.

But present.

Richard turned from the window.

"Gear check," he said.

Ashton nodded once. "Already started."

The equipment laid out on the table reflected the restrictions they had been given.

Minimal.

Intentional.

Each item had been reviewed, approved, and in some cases, reduced further by the Elyndoran officials before being returned to them.

No heavy scanning devices.

No powered mapping systems.

No environmental disruptors.

What remained was simple.

Field packs.

Basic navigation tools.

Non-lethal defense equipment.

Medical supplies.

Climbing line.

Water filtration units.

And a few compact devices allowed under strict limitation.

Dooley picked up one of the packs and weighed it in his hands.

"This feels… light."

"It's supposed to," Ashton said.

"I know, but usually when something important is happening, we bring more things."

"This time," Ashton said, "we bring fewer things and think more."

Dooley considered that.

"I see potential problems with that plan."

Milo gave the faintest hint of a smile.

Richard checked the fastening on his own pack, then moved to the central table.

"No changes once we leave," he said. "What we carry now is what we carry in."

Ashton nodded. "Agreed."

A soft knock sounded at the door.

Richard looked up.

"Come in."

The door opened.

Lydia stood there.

Serana just behind her.

But this time—

There was no hesitation.

No question.

Only readiness.

"We are prepared," Lydia said.

Her tone was calm.

Certain.

Richard stepped aside. "So are we."

She entered, her gaze moving immediately to the table, to the gear, to the arrangement of items. She took it in quickly, efficiently.

"You have followed the restrictions," she said.

Ashton inclined her head. "We were advised to."

Lydia nodded once.

"Good."

Serana moved along the wall, her attention scanning the room automatically before settling into a position where she could observe without interfering.

Lydia reached out and adjusted one of the packs slightly.

"This is too exposed," she said, repositioning a piece of equipment. "Branches will catch it."

She moved to another.

"This should be wrapped."

Her hands were precise.

Confident.

Not tentative.

Richard watched her for a moment.

"You've done this before," he said.

Lydia shook her head.

"No."

She finished securing the pack.

"I have studied those who have."

That answered the question in a different way.

Dooley leaned slightly toward Milo. "I feel like we just got a quiet upgrade."

Milo nodded. "Yes."

Ashton watched Lydia work, then said, "What's the first mistake we're likely to make?"

Lydia didn't look up.

"Moving too quickly."

She secured the final strap and stepped back.

"You will want to make progress," she said. "To follow the map. To reach the next marker."

She met Ashton's gaze.

"That will lead you into trouble."

Ashton nodded once. "Then we don't rush."

"No," Lydia said. "You don't."

Serana spoke quietly.

"You observe first," she said. "Then decide."

Richard nodded. "We stay together. No one moves ahead alone."

"Good," Lydia said.

There was a pause.

Then Dooley raised a hand slightly.

"Question."

Lydia looked at him.

"If something goes wrong," he said, "what's the first thing we do?"

Lydia considered that.

Then answered simply.

"We stop."

Dooley blinked.

"That's it?"

"That is the most important thing," she said. "The forest becomes dangerous when you continue without understanding."

Serana added, "And when you separate."

Milo nodded slowly.

"That makes sense."

Richard looked at each of them.

"Then that's our first rule."

No one disagreed.

Minister Halvern's voice came from the corridor.

"It is time."

The room shifted.

Not dramatically.

But enough.

Richard lifted his pack.

"Let's go."

The outer terraces were brighter now.

The sun had fully risen, casting long, clear light across the city. The pathways were more active, though still calm, still measured. People moved with purpose, but without urgency, as if time here followed a different set of expectations.

The transport waited where it had the day before.

But this time, it was not taking them to the court.

It was taking them away from it.

Lydia took her place without hesitation.

Serana positioned herself just behind and slightly to the side.

The cadets followed.

The transport began to move.

The city unfolded again around them—but now Richard saw it differently.

Not as something new.

But as something they were leaving behind.

Dooley leaned slightly toward the edge of the vehicle, watching as the structures began to thin.

"This is the last comfortable seat we're going to have for a while, isn't it?"

"Yes," Ashton said.

"I thought so."

Milo's gaze remained fixed on the horizon.

The forest line was closer now.

No longer distant.

No longer abstract.

Real.

The transport moved steadily, leaving the central district behind, passing through outer terraces where the structures gave way gradually to more open land. The transition was subtle at first.

Then it wasn't.

The greenery changed.

Less structured.

Less guided.

More… natural.

Untouched.

Ahead, the boundary came into view.

Not a wall.

Not a barrier.

A line.

Marked by a series of simple posts and a change in the land itself.

On one side—

The kingdom.

On the other—

The forest.

The transport slowed.

Then stopped.

No one spoke.

For a moment, the only sound was the faint movement of wind through the nearby growth.

Lydia stood.

Serana followed.

Richard rose as well.

The others with him.

They stepped down from the transport together.

The ground felt different.

Softer.

Less controlled.

Minister Halvern remained by the vehicle.

"This is as far as we go," he said.

His tone was calm.

But final.

Lydia nodded.

"We understand."

Halvern looked at the group.

"Once you cross," he said, "you are under the terms agreed upon. You carry our trust with you."

Richard inclined his head. "We will honor that."

Halvern nodded once.

Then stepped back.

No ceremony.

No signal.

Just space.

Lydia turned toward the forest.

For a moment, she did not move.

Neither did anyone else.

The trees stood close together just beyond the boundary, their canopy thick, their interior shadowed. The light did not pass through cleanly. It filtered. Broke. Shifted.

It felt—

Different.

Even from here.

Lydia took a breath.

Not deep.

Not dramatic.

Just enough.

Then she stepped forward.

Across the line.

Serana followed.

Richard stepped next.

Then Ashton.

Dooley.

Milo.

The moment they crossed—

The world changed.

Not completely.

But enough to feel it.

The light dimmed slightly beneath the canopy.

The air cooled.

The sounds shifted.

Distant city noise faded almost immediately, replaced by something else.

Layered.

Subtle.

Alive.

Dooley looked back once.

The boundary was still there.

Clear.

Close.

But already—

It felt farther away.

He turned forward again.

"Alright," he said quietly.

"This is it."

Lydia didn't look back.

"No," she said.

"It's just the beginning."

And without another word—

They moved deeper into the forest.

Chapter 8 — The First Misstep

The forest did not close behind them.

But it felt like it did.

Only a few dozen steps in, the boundary line was no longer visible. The open light of the terraces faded into layered shadow, broken into shifting patterns by leaves and branches high above. The air cooled further, carrying the scent of damp earth and growing things, thick enough to notice but not unpleasant.

Different.

That was the word Richard kept returning to.

Not hostile.

Not yet.

But different enough that every instinct trained in controlled environments began quietly reassessing what it thought it understood.

They moved carefully.

Not quickly.

Just as Lydia had instructed.

Each step placed with intention, each movement measured against what lay ahead rather than what had been left behind.

For a time, no one spoke.

There was too much to take in.

The forest was not silent.

Far from it.

Small sounds layered over one another—distant movement, the subtle rustle of leaves, something shifting along the branches above them, the faint call of unseen creatures moving deeper within the canopy. None of it formed a single pattern. It was a constant, low conversation that never fully revealed its source.

Dooley finally broke the silence.

"Okay," he said quietly, "this is… a lot."

Ashton nodded slightly. "Sensory overload."

"That's the phrase I was looking for."

Milo's gaze moved upward, following something along the branches that none of the others had noticed.

"It's not random," he said softly.

Richard glanced at him. "What do you mean?"

"The sounds," Milo said. "They repeat. Not exactly, but close."

Lydia slowed.

Then stopped.

The group followed immediately.

"What you're hearing," she said, "is layered activity."

Dooley frowned slightly. "That sounds like something Ashton would say."

Ashton didn't respond.

She was listening.

Lydia continued.

"Different species," she said. "Different movement patterns. Some are reacting to us. Some are reacting to each other."

She turned slightly, scanning the surrounding trees.

"And some," she added, "are simply part of the forest's normal rhythm."

Dooley shifted his weight slightly.

"So how do we know which is which?"

Lydia looked at him.

"You don't," she said.

There it was again.

The same answer.

Not what he wanted.

But consistent.

Serana stepped forward slightly, her attention focused on the ground ahead.

"We move," she said quietly. "But we move with awareness."

Richard nodded once. "Stay close."

They continued.

The terrain changed subtly as they moved deeper.

The ground, firm at first, began to soften slightly underfoot. Roots crossed their path in irregular patterns, some exposed, some hidden just beneath the surface. Low vegetation thickened, forcing them to adjust their path more often than the map would have suggested.

Richard kept one eye on the terrain and one on Lydia.

She moved with care.

Not hesitantly.

But attentively.

Each step placed after consideration, not assumption.

She wasn't guessing.

She was interpreting.

After several minutes, Ashton spoke.

"We should be nearing the first marker."

Lydia slowed again.

"Show me."

Ashton brought up the map projection, keeping it low and dim so it didn't disrupt the surrounding light. She aligned it with their estimated position.

"The river bend should be ahead," she said. "Based on the angle of entry and the direction we've maintained."

Milo glanced toward the right.

"There's a slope there," he said. "Ground dips slightly."

Richard followed his gaze.

He could see it now.

Subtle.

But present.

Lydia nodded.

"Yes," she said. "That matches."

They adjusted their course slightly.

The sound reached them before the sight.

Water.

Not loud.

But steady.

Dooley's expression lifted slightly. "That's encouraging."

Ashton nodded. "First confirmation."

They moved toward it carefully.

The trees began to thin just enough to allow more light through, and within moments, the river came into view.

It curved gently through the forest, its surface broken by small ripples and occasional protruding stones. The banks were uneven, lined with thick vegetation that leaned inward toward the water.

Richard studied it.

"This matches."

Ashton checked the projection again. "Within acceptable variation."

Milo crouched slightly near the edge, examining the ground.

"Tracks," he said.

Dooley leaned slightly closer. "Animal?"

"Yes."

"What kind?"

Milo shook his head slightly. "Not sure."

Lydia stepped closer, kneeling beside him.

She studied the impressions carefully.

"River antelope," she said. "Recent."

Dooley nodded slowly. "That sounds safe."

"They are," Lydia said. "Mostly."

"Mostly?"

"They flee when startled," she said. "But if cornered—"

"Right," Dooley said quickly. "We won't corner anything."

Serana's gaze moved along the opposite bank.

"We cross here?" she asked.

Lydia stood.

She looked at the river.

Then at the surrounding area.

Then back at the map.

"This is where he marked the bend," she said.

Richard nodded. "Then we cross."

Lydia didn't move.

Something in her expression shifted slightly.

Not uncertainty.

Evaluation.

"This is where he noticed the river," she said.

Ashton frowned slightly. "What's the difference?"

Lydia looked at her.

"The map shows where he paid attention," she said. "Not necessarily where he made the best choice."

The group quieted.

Richard looked at the river again.

Then at Lydia.

"You think this might not be the crossing point."

"I think we should confirm," she said.

Serana nodded once. "We don't assume."

Dooley exhaled softly. "We confirm."

Ashton adjusted the projection slightly. "The next marker is… unclear."

"That's consistent," Richard said.

Milo stood slowly.

"The ground upstream is firmer," he said. "Less erosion."

Lydia looked in that direction.

Then back at the river.

Then at the map.

She made a decision.

"We move upstream," she said.

No hesitation.

Richard nodded. "Alright."

They followed the river's edge, moving carefully along the bank. The terrain shifted slightly as they went, the ground becoming more stable, the vegetation less dense in places where the water had carved a more defined path.

After several minutes, the river narrowed slightly.

The current slowed.

And a series of natural stones formed a crossing point.

Not perfect.

But manageable.

Lydia stopped.

"This is better."

Serana stepped forward, testing the first stone with her weight.

Stable.

She moved to the next.

Then the next.

Each step deliberate.

She reached the far side and turned.

"Clear."

Richard gestured. "One at a time."

Milo went next.

Then Ashton.

Then Dooley, who paused halfway across.

"This is fine," he said. "This is completely fine."

"Keep moving," Ashton said.

"I am moving."

He stepped onto the final stone and reached the far side.

Richard crossed last.

When he stepped onto solid ground again, he turned briefly to look back.

The river curved away behind them.

Already partially hidden by the trees.

Already less distinct.

They had made their first decision.

And it had not come from the map.

Richard looked at Lydia.

She met his gaze.

A small nod.

Not pride.

Not relief.

Just confirmation.

They had chosen carefully.

And it had mattered.

Dooley adjusted his pack slightly.

"Well," he said quietly, "that was our first official 'don't trust the map' moment."

Ashton nodded. "There will be more."

Milo glanced deeper into the forest.

"There already are."

Richard turned forward.

The terrain ahead thickened again, the light dimming slightly as the canopy closed more tightly above them.

"Stay sharp," he said.

Lydia stepped forward.

Serana beside her.

The others followed.

Behind them, the river faded from sight.

Ahead—

The forest deepened.

And the map—

Was already beginning to fall short.

Chapter 9 — The First Relic

The forest thickened.

Not suddenly.

Not in a way that forced them to stop.

But steadily enough that, after a short time, Richard realized the space around them had changed again.

The trees stood closer now.

Their trunks rose tall and straight, their upper branches interlocking to form a canopy that allowed only scattered light to reach the ground below. What light did pass through arrived in broken shafts, shifting gently as the leaves above moved in the unseen currents of air.

The ground followed suit.

Roots crossed more frequently, some rising high enough to step over, others twisting just beneath the surface where they could not be seen until the last moment. The undergrowth thickened in patches, forcing the group to adjust their path again and again, never quite moving in a straight line for long.

Progress slowed.

Not dramatically.

But enough to notice.

No one complained.

They had already learned that moving quickly was not the goal.

Moving correctly was.

Lydia led.

Not far ahead.

Just enough to set the pace.

Serana remained slightly behind and to her side, her attention divided between the path ahead and the space behind them. Every few steps, her gaze shifted—left, right, upward—never lingering long, but never missing much.

Richard walked just behind Lydia.

Ashton and Milo followed close together.

Dooley brought up the rear, though not by design—he simply had a habit of falling slightly behind when he was taking everything in.

"This place keeps changing," he said quietly.

"It's not changing," Ashton replied. "We are."

Dooley considered that.

"I don't like that answer as much."

Milo glanced at the ground, then back ahead.

"The spacing is tighter," he said. "More growth."

Lydia nodded without turning.

"Yes," she said. "We are moving toward an older section."

Richard looked around again.

Older.

He could see it now.

Not in any single tree.

But in the way everything fit together.

Nothing here looked newly grown.

Nothing looked recently disturbed.

The forest had settled into itself long ago.

They continued for several more minutes before Lydia slowed.

Then stopped.

The others followed immediately.

"What is it?" Richard asked quietly.

Lydia didn't answer right away.

Her gaze had fixed on something just ahead and slightly to the right.

She stepped carefully in that direction.

Serana moved with her.

The others followed at a distance of a few steps.

At first, Richard didn't see anything unusual.

Just more of the same—roots, low plants, scattered leaves.

Then the angle shifted.

And something broke the pattern.

A shape.

Partially buried.

Not natural.

Lydia knelt slowly.

Her hand hovered just above the surface, not touching.

"Here," she said softly.

The others moved closer.

Ashton crouched beside her, brushing away a thin layer of loose debris.

The object emerged gradually.

Stone.

Worked.

Not shaped by erosion, but by intention.

A small carving.

Simple, but precise.

Lines etched into its surface formed a pattern that curved and intersected in ways that felt deliberate, though not immediately understandable.

Dooley leaned in.

"That wasn't here by accident."

"No," Lydia said.

She studied it carefully, her eyes moving across the markings.

Recognition began to form.

Richard could see it in her expression.

"This is River Tribe work," she said.

Milo tilted his head slightly. "How can you tell?"

Lydia traced the air just above the carving, following one of the curved lines.

"These patterns," she said. "They represent movement—water, current, flow. The River Tribe uses them to mark places of significance along waterways."

Ashton glanced toward the direction they had come.

"The river we crossed."

"Yes."

Lydia nodded.

"This would have been near a known path."

Dooley looked around.

"So… we're standing in someone's space."

"Not exactly," Lydia said.

She looked up, scanning the area.

"This is not a settlement marker," she said. "It's more like a sign… or a reminder."

Serana's voice came quietly.

"Meaning we should be cautious."

Lydia nodded once.

"Yes."

Richard studied the surroundings more carefully now.

Nothing had changed.

And yet—

Everything felt slightly different.

"Do we leave it?" he asked.

Lydia didn't answer immediately.

She looked back at the carving.

Then at the ground around it.

Then at the map in Ashton's hand.

"It is not in a sacred formation," she said slowly. "It is not part of a structure."

She paused.

"It was likely displaced over time."

Ashton raised an eyebrow slightly. "So it's allowed?"

"Possibly," Lydia said.

The word hung there.

Dooley shifted slightly. "That doesn't sound certain."

"It isn't," Lydia said.

There it was.

The first moment.

The one where knowledge met reality and did not fully resolve.

Richard watched her carefully.

"You don't know for sure," he said.

Lydia met his gaze.

"No."

No defensiveness.

No hesitation.

Just truth.

Serana stepped slightly closer.

"Then we leave it," she said.

Simple.

Final.

Lydia looked at the carving again.

For a moment, something passed across her expression.

Not disappointment.

Not frustration.

Understanding.

Then she nodded.

"Yes."

She rose slowly.

Ashton brushed the remaining debris lightly back into place, covering the carving just enough to return it to how they had found it.

Dooley exhaled quietly.

"That feels like the right call."

Milo nodded. "It is."

Richard glanced at Lydia.

She had stepped back slightly, her gaze still resting on the spot.

"You wanted to bring it back," he said.

It wasn't an accusation.

Just an observation.

Lydia nodded once.

"Yes."

She looked at him.

"But wanting is not the same as knowing."

That landed.

Ashton gave a small nod. "Good distinction."

Lydia turned away from the carving.

"We move on," she said.

No hesitation now.

They resumed their path.

But something had changed.

Not the forest.

Not the mission.

The understanding.

Dooley walked a little closer to Milo this time.

"So," he said quietly, "lesson one—just because you find something doesn't mean you take it."

Milo nodded. "Yes."

"Lesson two—if Lydia says 'possibly,' we treat it like 'no.'"

Ashton glanced back. "That's actually useful."

"I try."

Richard walked in silence for a few steps.

Then spoke.

"That was the right call."

Lydia nodded.

"I know."

But her voice carried something new.

Not uncertainty.

Not doubt.

Weight.

The kind that came from making a choice and understanding what it meant.

Ahead, the forest continued.

Unchanged.

Unyielding.

But now—

They understood it just a little more.

And that understanding had cost them something small.

Which meant—

It would matter when the cost was not small.

Richard looked forward.

"Stay focused," he said.

The group adjusted slightly.

Tighter.

More aware.

Behind them, the hidden carving remained where it had been for years.

Undisturbed.

Respected.

Ahead—

The path narrowed.

And the forest—

Watched.

Chapter 10 — The Silent Stalker

The forest grew quieter.

Not completely.

Never completely.

But enough that the change could be felt before it was fully understood.

At first, it was subtle.

The layered sounds that had followed them since entering—the distant calls, the shifting movement in the branches, the low rustle of unseen creatures—began to thin. Not vanish, but pull back, as if something had passed through the area ahead of them and everything else had chosen, quietly and instinctively, to give it space.

Richard noticed it first.

He slowed slightly.

Not enough to stop the group.

But enough to change the rhythm.

Behind him, Ashton caught the shift immediately.

"What is it?" she asked quietly.

Richard didn't answer right away.

He listened.

The forest was still speaking.

But not in the same way.

"It changed," he said.

Milo nodded from just behind Ashton.

"Yes."

Dooley glanced around.

"Changed how?"

Before anyone else could answer, Serana raised one hand.

Not high.

Not sharply.

Just enough.

The group stopped.

Immediately.

No hesitation.

No questions.

That alone told Richard everything he needed to know.

Serana had felt it too.

Lydia stood still beside her, her gaze moving slowly across the trees, not searching for something obvious, but reading what was no longer there.

"The smaller animals have moved away," she said quietly.

Dooley blinked. "All of them?"

"Enough," Lydia replied.

Serana stepped forward slightly.

Her posture shifted.

Not tense.

But ready.

"Stay close," she said.

Her voice was low.

Controlled.

Richard nodded once. "Together."

The group tightened instinctively.

Not crowding.

But closer.

Aware.

Serana moved a few steps ahead now, her attention focused forward, but her awareness extending in all directions. Every step she took was deliberate, her weight placed carefully, her movement quiet enough that even the forest seemed to accept it.

Richard followed just behind Lydia.

Ashton and Milo stayed close.

Dooley kept his voice down this time.

"So," he said softly, "this is the part where something is watching us."

Ashton didn't dismiss it.

"That is likely," she said.

"That is not comforting."

"It's accurate."

Milo's gaze moved upward briefly, then back down.

"Not above," he said.

Richard glanced at him. "Ground level?"

Milo nodded once.

"Or just above it."

Serana stopped again.

This time more abruptly.

The group halted.

No one spoke.

The silence settled deeper now.

Not empty.

Focused.

Serana crouched slightly, her eyes fixed on the ground a few paces ahead.

Richard followed her line of sight.

At first, he saw nothing.

Then—

He did.

A shape in the soil.

Not clear.

But present.

A depression.

Then another.

And another.

Tracks.

Large.

Set wide apart.

Lydia stepped forward slowly, stopping just behind Serana.

She didn't kneel.

Didn't touch.

She simply observed.

Her voice was barely above a whisper.

"Shadowpanther."

Dooley's breath caught slightly.

"That sounds… not friendly."

"It isn't," Lydia said.

Ashton leaned in slightly, careful not to disturb the ground.

"How recent?"

Serana answered.

"Recent enough."

That was not a measure.

It was a warning.

Richard scanned the surrounding trees again.

Nothing moved.

Nothing revealed itself.

And yet—

The absence of sound had deepened.

As if the forest itself was holding still.

"Is it following us?" Dooley asked quietly.

Lydia didn't answer.

Serana did.

"Possibly."

"That is also not comforting."

"No," Serana said. "It isn't."

She rose slowly.

"Predators like this do not rush," she continued. "They observe. They wait."

Richard nodded.

"Then we don't give it a reason."

Ashton glanced at him. "Meaning?"

"Meaning we stay together," Richard said. "No sudden movement. No separation."

Milo added quietly, "No running."

Dooley looked at him. "I was just thinking about running."

"Don't."

"Right."

Serana stepped slightly to the side, adjusting their formation without calling attention to it.

"Closer," she said.

They moved in.

Not tightly packed.

But within reach.

Within awareness.

Lydia's voice came softly.

"It will test us."

Richard glanced at her. "How?"

"By waiting," she said.

Ashton frowned slightly. "That's not much of a test."

"It is," Lydia said. "Because waiting creates uncertainty."

She met Ashton's gaze.

"And uncertainty leads to mistakes."

That landed.

Richard felt it immediately.

The instinct to act.

To move.

To resolve the unknown.

That was the danger.

Serana began to move again.

Slowly.

Deliberately.

The group followed.

Each step measured.

Each movement controlled.

The forest remained quiet.

Too quiet.

Minutes passed.

Or maybe less.

Time stretched differently here.

Then—

A sound.

Soft.

To the left.

Not loud.

But distinct.

A shift in leaves.

A weight moving just out of sight.

Dooley froze.

Completely.

Ashton's eyes snapped in that direction.

Milo didn't move at all.

Serana stopped.

Her head turned slightly.

Not quickly.

Not sharply.

Just enough.

Richard held his position.

He could feel it now.

Not see it.

But feel it.

Presence.

Close.

Watching.

Lydia's voice came quietly.

"Do not look directly for it."

Dooley blinked. "What?"

"It sees that as a challenge," she said.

"That seems unfair."

"Most predators are."

Serana shifted her stance slightly.

Not aggressive.

Not defensive.

Balanced.

Prepared.

Another sound.

This time behind them.

Not closer.

But not distant either.

Ashton spoke under her breath.

"It's circling."

Milo nodded once.

"Yes."

Richard exhaled slowly.

"Then we keep moving."

Serana gave a slight nod.

"Forward."

They moved again.

Slow.

Controlled.

Together.

The sounds followed.

Never fully revealing.

Never fully disappearing.

A step to the left.

A shift behind.

A presence just beyond sight.

Dooley kept his voice barely audible.

"I would like to formally state that I do not enjoy this."

"No one does," Ashton said.

"That makes me feel slightly better."

Lydia remained focused ahead.

"It will leave," she said quietly.

Dooley blinked again. "You sound very confident about that."

"It will leave," she repeated.

"When it understands we are not prey."

Richard glanced at her. "And how do we show that?"

Lydia didn't look at him.

"By not acting like prey."

That was it.

Simple.

Difficult.

Clear.

They continued forward.

Step by step.

No sudden movement.

No break in formation.

No panic.

The forest held its breath around them.

Then—

Gradually—

The sound shifted.

Not gone.

But changing.

The tension eased slightly.

The layered sounds of the forest began to return.

First one.

Then another.

Then many.

The quiet lifted.

Not completely.

But enough.

Serana slowed.

Then stopped.

She listened.

Longer this time.

Then straightened.

"It's gone," she said.

Dooley let out a breath he had been holding for far too long. "Good," he said. "I very much prefer when things are gone."

Ashton relaxed slightly.

"Or at least not actively evaluating us as food."

Milo looked back once.

Then forward again.

"It's still nearby," he said.

Serana nodded.

"Yes."

Lydia turned slightly toward the group.

"It will remember us," she said.

Dooley blinked again. "That does not sound reassuring."

"It isn't meant to be."

Richard looked at each of them.

"No one panicked," he said.

That mattered.

Ashton nodded. "We held formation."

Milo added quietly, "We listened."

Dooley gave a small, uncertain smile. "We did not run."

"That too," Richard said.

Lydia met his gaze.

"That is how you move through this forest," she said.

"Not by overcoming it."

"By understanding it."

Richard nodded once.

"Then we keep doing that."

Serana stepped forward again.

"Move."

They followed.

The forest resumed its rhythm around them.

Alive.

Layered.

Watching.

But now—

They understood something they hadn't before.

They were not alone here.

And they were not the most capable presence in the forest.

Not even close.

Richard looked ahead.

"Stay sharp," he said quietly.

The group moved deeper.

And the forest—

Let them pass.

Chapter 11 — The First Night

They did not travel after dark.

But they felt it coming.

The light had been fading for some time—not quickly, not in any sudden shift, but gradually, as the canopy above thickened and the angle of the sun changed. The broken shafts of light that had once reached the forest floor became thinner, less frequent, until the ground beneath them settled into a softer, more even dimness.

Lydia slowed.

Then stopped.

"We stay here," she said.

No one questioned it.

Richard looked around, taking in the space.

It wasn't open.

Not exactly.

But it was less dense than the surrounding area. The trees stood slightly farther apart, and the ground, while still uneven, offered enough room for them to gather without crowding into one another.

Serana moved immediately, circling the area with quiet efficiency. Her gaze moved across the perimeter, checking lines of sight, identifying anything that might shift unexpectedly once darkness settled in.

"Good enough," she said after a moment.

That was as close to approval as she ever needed to give.

Dooley set his pack down carefully.

"So this is it," he said. "First night."

Ashton glanced upward, where the last traces of filtered light clung to the canopy. "It will get darker than this."

"That is not surprising," Dooley said. "But I appreciate the confirmation."

Milo moved to the edge of the clearing, crouching briefly to examine the ground.

"No recent tracks," he said. "At least nothing large."

Serana nodded once.

"That will change," she said.

Dooley straightened slowly. "You have a very consistent way of saying things that are not comforting."

Serana did not respond.

Richard set his pack down and began unpacking what little they had brought for rest. There was no elaborate setup. No tents. No structures. Just simple ground coverings, arranged close enough to maintain awareness of one another without forming a tight cluster.

Lydia moved more slowly.

Not uncertain.

But thoughtful.

She looked around the clearing again, her gaze lingering on the surrounding trees, the spacing, the direction of the wind as it shifted faintly through the upper branches.

"This will work," she said quietly.

It wasn't confidence.

It was acceptance.

The difference mattered.

As the last of the light faded, the forest changed again.

Not into silence.

Never silence.

But into something deeper.

The sounds shifted—lower, more deliberate, spaced differently. What had once been scattered and overlapping now seemed to move in patterns that were harder to follow, as if the forest spoke more softly at night, but with greater intention.

Dooley sat back on his hands and looked around.

"Okay," he said, keeping his voice low, "this is definitely different."

Ashton nodded. "Night cycle."

"That's a very technical way to describe something that feels like it's watching us."

Milo glanced at him.

"It was watching us before."

"That is not helping."

Richard allowed himself a small breath.

"Eat," he said. "Then we rest in turns."

No one argued.

They ate simply.

Compact rations.

Water carefully measured and filtered.

No fire.

That had been made clear before they entered.

The forest did not permit unnecessary disruption.

Dooley chewed thoughtfully for a moment.

"I miss warm food," he said.

"You always miss warm food," Ashton replied.

"Yes," Dooley said. "Because warm food is consistently better."

Milo sat quietly, finishing his portion without comment, his attention drifting occasionally to the edges of the clearing.

Lydia ate more slowly.

Not because she was distracted.

Because she was thinking.

Richard noticed.

"You're reviewing," he said.

She looked at him.

"Yes."

"The map?"

"And the day."

She paused.

"They are not the same."

Richard nodded once.

"No," he said. "They're not."

Lydia set her food aside.

"For a long time," she said, "I thought understanding the forest meant knowing its patterns."

She looked out into the darkness beyond the clearing.

"The types of plants. The movement of animals. The structure of the land."

She paused.

"That is part of it."

"But not all," Ashton said.

Lydia nodded.

"Not all."

Dooley leaned slightly forward.

"So what's the rest?"

Lydia considered the question.

Then answered carefully.

"Knowing when you don't understand what you're seeing."

That settled over them.

Milo nodded slightly.

"That happened today."

"Yes," Lydia said.

"The river," Richard said.

"And the carving," Ashton added.

Lydia looked at her.

"Yes."

There was no hesitation now.

No uncertainty.

Just clarity.

Serana, standing near the edge of the clearing, spoke without turning.

"That awareness keeps you alive," she said.

Dooley nodded slowly.

"I am beginning to appreciate that."

Richard leaned back slightly, resting his arms across his knees.

"We did well," he said.

Not praise.

Assessment.

Ashton nodded. "We adapted."

Milo added quietly, "We didn't force anything."

Dooley smiled faintly. "And we didn't get eaten."

"That also counts," Ashton said.

A faint shift in the air moved through the clearing.

Cooler now.

Night fully settled.

Above them, through small breaks in the canopy, the faintest points of light appeared—stars, distant and partially obscured, but present.

Dooley looked up.

"I always forget they're still there," he said.

"They don't go anywhere," Ashton replied.

"I know. It just feels like they do."

Milo followed his gaze briefly.

Then lowered it again.

"The forest changes what you notice."

Lydia nodded.

"Yes."

She looked at the small opening above them.

"For me," she said, "the stars always meant distance."

She paused.

"Now they feel… farther."

Richard considered that.

Then nodded.

"I understand."

There was a quiet moment.

Not empty.

Just still.

Serana stepped closer.

"Rotation," she said.

Richard nodded. "I'll take first watch."

Milo looked at him. "I'll take second."

Ashton glanced up. "I'll take third."

Dooley raised a hand slightly. "I will take fourth, with enthusiasm and moderate alertness."

Serana gave the faintest hint of approval.

"I'll remain awake," she said.

Dooley blinked. "All night?"

"Yes."

"That seems… impressive."

"It is necessary."

Lydia shook her head slightly.

"You should rest," she said.

Serana looked at her.

"I will," she said.

It was not an argument.

It was a statement.

Lydia didn't push further.

She understood.

Richard settled into position near the edge of the clearing, his back against one of the larger roots, his gaze moving steadily across the darkened forest.

The others lay down one by one.

Not deeply relaxed.

But willing to rest.

Lydia remained seated for a moment longer.

Looking out into the forest.

Thinking.

Then she lay down as well.

Serana moved quietly along the perimeter.

Never still.

Never distracted.

The forest continued its quiet conversation around them.

Not threatening.

But never absent.

Richard watched.

Listened.

Time passed.

Slowly.

Steadily.

And as the first night settled fully around them, one thing became clear.

They had entered the forest.

But they had not yet begun to understand it.

And the deeper they went—

The more it would ask of them.

Richard adjusted his position slightly, his gaze still moving, still attentive.

"Stay sharp," he said quietly to himself.

The forest did not answer.

But it listened.

Chapter 12 — The Path That Wasn't There

Morning did not arrive all at once.

It returned in layers.

A faint lifting of darkness beneath the canopy. A slow softening of shadow. The quiet reappearance of distant sound—first one voice, then another, until the forest began speaking again in its daytime rhythm.

Richard Taylor noticed it before he opened his eyes.

The change.

Not brighter.

Not clearer.

Just… different.

He sat up slowly.

The clearing remained dim, but no longer shadowed in the same way. Shapes that had been uncertain in the night were now defined again—trees, roots, the uneven ground where they had rested.

Serana stood at the edge of the clearing.

Exactly where she had been.

Her posture unchanged.

Her attention outward.

Richard rose and stepped closer.

"You didn't sleep," he said quietly.

"I rested," she replied.

He didn't press.

Behind them, the others began to stir.

Dooley stretched and immediately winced.

"I have discovered new muscles," he said. "And they are not pleased."

"That means you slept," Ashton replied without opening her eyes.

"That is not how I would describe it."

Milo sat up quietly, his gaze already moving toward the edges of the clearing.

"The sounds are back," he said.

Lydia rose more slowly.

She took a moment to look around before speaking.

"Yes," she said. "Day movement."

She stepped forward slightly, her attention moving across the trees, the spacing, the direction of light filtering through the canopy.

"This area is stable," she added. "For now."

Dooley blinked. "For now?"

Lydia glanced at him.

"It changes," she said.

That had become familiar.

And not entirely reassuring.

They packed quickly.

No unnecessary movement.

No wasted time.

What they had brought was already minimal. What they carried now was exactly the same as the day before—nothing added, nothing removed.

Richard checked the group.

"All good?"

Ashton nodded. "Ready."

Milo gave a small nod.

Dooley lifted his pack. "As ready as I am going to be."

Lydia stepped forward.

"Then we move."

The forest felt different in the morning.

Not safer.

But more visible.

The patterns of movement returned, though not fully predictable. Birds moved in the upper branches, small creatures crossed unseen paths beneath the undergrowth, and the shifting light made it easier to distinguish depth from shadow.

For a time, their progress was steady.

They followed the direction established the day before, adjusting for terrain, keeping formation, allowing Lydia to guide their pace.

The map remained present.

But less dominant.

That shift was subtle.

But important.

Ashton noticed it first.

"We're not checking it as often," she said.

Richard glanced at her. "We don't need to yet."

"That will change."

"Yes."

Milo walked slightly ahead for a few steps, then stopped.

The others halted immediately.

"What is it?" Richard asked.

Milo pointed toward the ground ahead.

"Trail."

Richard stepped forward.

There it was.

Faint.

But visible.

A narrow break in the undergrowth, where something—or someone—had passed repeatedly enough to leave a pattern.

Dooley leaned in slightly.

"That looks promising."

Ashton frowned.

"Or misleading."

Lydia stepped forward.

She studied the trail carefully.

Not just the path itself.

But the surrounding area.

The spacing of the trees.

The type of growth.

The direction of the light.

"This is not his path," she said.

Dooley blinked. "It looks like a path."

"Yes," Lydia said. "But not his."

Milo nodded slightly. "Too consistent."

Ashton glanced at him. "Meaning?"

"Used often," Milo said. "Not recently made."

Lydia looked at the trail again.

"This could be a tribal route," she said quietly.

That changed everything.

Dooley stepped back instinctively.

"Okay," he said, "then we definitely don't follow that."

Serana's voice came low.

"No."

Richard nodded.

"We avoid it."

Lydia remained still for a moment longer.

Then stepped back.

"We go around."

The terrain shifted again as they altered course.

The ground rose slightly, then dipped, forcing them to navigate a series of uneven ridges and shallow depressions. The vegetation thickened in patches, then thinned again without clear pattern.

The map offered little help.

The next marker—

Was unclear.

Ashton activated the projection briefly.

"This section," she said, "is one of the vague ones."

Dooley nodded. "I remember. 'Large tree.'"

"Yes," Ashton said. "That's all it says."

Richard looked around.

There were many large trees.

More than many.

Most of them.

"That's not useful," Dooley added.

"It's what we have," Ashton said.

Lydia stepped forward slowly.

Her gaze moved upward.

Not across the ground.

Into the canopy.

Richard followed her line of sight.

At first, he didn't see anything different.

Then—

He did.

One tree.

Slightly different.

Its bark lighter.

Not white.

But pale compared to the others.

Its branches spread wider, catching more light.

Lydia moved toward it.

Carefully.

Serana followed.

The others stayed close.

When they reached it, Lydia placed her hand lightly against the trunk.

"This is the one," she said.

Ashton checked the map again.

"That aligns," she said.

Milo looked around the base of the tree.

"No clear markings," he said.

Dooley glanced at the trunk.

"So we just… trust that this is the correct large tree?"

Lydia shook her head.

"We confirm."

She stepped back.

And looked beyond it.

That was the difference.

Not stopping at the marker.

Looking past it.

"The next direction," she said slowly, "should be toward rising ground."

Richard turned.

The terrain ahead did rise.

Subtly.

But enough.

"That fits," he said.

Ashton nodded. "Agreed."

Dooley smiled slightly. "We are getting better at this."

Lydia didn't return the smile.

"We are learning," she said.

"Not mastering."

That mattered.

They moved on.

The forest changed again.

More sharply this time.

The ground became uneven.

Not just with roots.

With growth.

Plants spread thicker here, their leaves broader, their colors deeper. Some rose waist-high, others climbed along trunks, forming dense patterns that blocked clear passage.

Progress slowed.

Again.

Dooley pushed gently through a cluster of low branches.

"This is getting… complicated."

Ashton moved more carefully.

"Watch where you step."

Milo stopped.

Again.

The others froze.

"What is it?" Richard asked.

Milo pointed.

To the ground.

A cluster of plants.

Small.

Bright.

Almost inviting.

Lydia stepped forward quickly.

"Don't touch that," she said.

Dooley froze mid-step.

"I wasn't going to."

"You were thinking about it."

"…maybe."

Lydia crouched slightly, examining the plant.

"False Sunberries," she said.

Dooley blinked. "Those look exactly like the safe ones."

"Yes."

"That seems unfair."

"They cause severe dehydration," Lydia said.

"That is extremely unfair."

Ashton nodded. "Good to know."

Milo stepped back slightly.

"They're everywhere here."

Lydia looked around.

She was right.

The plants spread across the ground in clusters, blending with other growth in a way that made them difficult to distinguish at a glance.

"This area is deceptive," Lydia said.

Serana nodded once.

"Careful movement."

Richard adjusted his stance.

"Single file," he said. "Follow Lydia's path exactly."

No one argued.

They moved slowly.

Deliberately.

Each step placed where Lydia stepped.

Each movement controlled.

The forest pressed closer here.

Not physically.

But perceptually.

The density.

The color.

The subtle hazards hidden among ordinary-looking growth.

Dooley kept his voice low.

"I liked the river better."

Ashton nodded. "The river was honest."

"This feels… less honest."

Milo glanced at the plants again.

"It's not trying to deceive," he said.

"It just is."

That was worse.

Richard looked ahead.

The terrain continued to rise.

The forest thickened.

And the map—

Offered less and less.

"Stay focused," he said quietly.

Lydia continued forward.

Serana beside her.

The others followed.

Behind them, the deceptive plants faded from view.

Ahead—

The forest grew more complex.

And the path—

Less certain.

Chapter 13 — When the Ground Shifts

The rise in terrain became more pronounced.

Not steep.

But persistent.

Each step carried them slightly higher, the ground beneath their feet shifting from soft, layered soil to something firmer in places, then back again without clear pattern. Roots gave way to stone, then disappeared again beneath dense growth, as if the forest itself had never fully decided what it wanted the land to be.

Richard felt it in his footing.

Subtle changes.

Small adjustments.

Nothing dangerous on its own.

But enough to require attention.

They moved in silence for a time.

Not out of caution alone.

But because the forest demanded it.

The deeper they went, the more it felt like something that should not be interrupted unnecessarily.

Dooley broke that silence eventually.

Quietly.

"I think I preferred when the map made more sense," he said.

Ashton didn't look up from her surroundings. "That was never the map."

"It felt like the map."

"That was confidence," she said. "Not accuracy."

Dooley considered that.

"I would like some of that confidence back."

Lydia slowed.

Then stopped.

The group halted immediately.

She didn't turn.

Didn't speak right away.

Her attention had shifted upward.

Richard followed her gaze.

The canopy.

Something had changed.

At first, it was difficult to see.

Then—

It wasn't.

The leaves were moving.

Not with the usual soft rhythm of airflow.

More irregular.

More unsettled.

Milo spoke quietly.

"Wind."

"Yes," Lydia said.

"But not from above."

That was the difference.

The movement wasn't passing over the forest.

It was moving through it.

Serana stepped forward slightly, her eyes scanning the upper branches, then the surrounding terrain.

"Pressure shift," she said.

Richard frowned slightly. "Storm?"

"Possibly."

Ashton looked at her tablet briefly, then back up.

"We don't have atmospheric data down here."

"No," Lydia said. "We wouldn't."

Dooley glanced around.

"I don't like the phrase 'pressure shift.'"

"It means we need to move carefully," Serana said.

"That part I understand."

The wind increased.

Not strong.

But noticeable.

It moved through the trees in uneven pulses, causing branches to sway in ways that felt less coordinated than before. Leaves rustled in layered waves, and the subtle sounds of the forest began to shift again.

Richard looked ahead.

"We keep moving?"

Lydia hesitated.

Not long.

But long enough to matter.

Then—

"Yes," she said.

"For now."

The forest responded quickly.

The ground beneath them changed.

More sharply this time.

Loose soil gave way to patches of exposed rock, then back again to softer ground that shifted slightly underfoot. The roots they stepped over felt less stable, some shifting just enough to force a correction in balance.

Dooley adjusted his footing carefully.

"Okay," he said quietly, "this is becoming less cooperative."

Ashton nodded. "The soil is loosening."

Milo crouched briefly, pressing his hand against the ground.

"It's not just loose," he said. "It's moving."

Richard felt it then.

Not movement like a slide.

But a subtle shift.

As if the layers beneath the surface were adjusting.

Lydia stopped again.

This time more firmly.

"We don't continue forward like this," she said.

Serana nodded once.

"Agreed."

Dooley looked around.

"So what do we do?"

Lydia turned slightly, scanning the surrounding terrain.

Her gaze moved across the slope, the spacing of the trees, the direction of the wind, the way the ground angled beneath the growth.

She wasn't looking for a path.

She was reading the land.

"The ridge," she said.

Richard followed her line of sight.

To the right.

A slightly higher line of ground.

Not steep.

But elevated enough that the soil appeared more compact.

"That's more stable," Ashton said.

"Yes," Lydia replied.

"But it takes us off the map."

That was the cost.

Dooley exhaled slowly.

"I am noticing a pattern."

Richard looked at Lydia.

"What's the risk?"

She met his gaze.

"We lose alignment with the drawn path."

"And the benefit?"

"We don't risk the ground failing beneath us."

That was not a difficult choice.

Richard nodded.

"We take the ridge."

No hesitation.

No debate.

Ashton adjusted her position immediately.

Milo rose and shifted with them.

Dooley followed.

"I support not falling through the ground," he said.

Serana moved first.

Testing.

Each step placed carefully, her weight shifting just enough to confirm stability before committing fully.

Lydia followed.

Then Richard.

Then the others.

The ridge held.

Not perfectly.

But better.

The ground felt firmer, the roots more anchored, the movement beneath the surface less pronounced.

The wind continued to move through the trees, but its effect here was less disruptive.

Dooley glanced back toward where they had been.

The lower ground looked the same.

But it didn't feel the same.

"I think that would have gone badly," he said.

Ashton nodded. "Eventually."

Milo looked ahead.

"The ridge curves."

Richard saw it.

It did.

Not sharply.

But enough to alter their direction.

"We're drifting," Ashton said.

"Yes," Lydia replied.

"That's the trade."

Richard considered it.

Then nodded.

"We stay safe first."

"Agreed," Ashton said.

The group continued along the ridge.

The forest shifted again as they moved.

The trees spaced slightly differently, the light filtering through in new patterns, the ground beneath them responding to a different structure than before.

But the map—

No longer matched.

Not cleanly.

Not clearly.

After several minutes, Lydia slowed again.

This time, she turned.

Looking back.

Then forward.

Then at the terrain around them.

"We need to reorient," she said.

Ashton activated the projection.

It hovered uncertainly between them.

"This is where we should be," she said, indicating a point.

Then she looked around.

"And this is where we are."

The two did not match.

Not anymore.

Dooley leaned in.

"That's not encouraging."

Milo studied the projection.

"We can recover," he said.

Lydia nodded.

"Yes."

But her voice carried something new.

Not doubt.

Not fear.

Awareness.

The map was no longer guiding them.

They were guiding themselves.

Richard looked at her.

"What do you need?"

Lydia met his gaze.

"Time," she said.

"To read this correctly."

Serana stepped slightly outward, her attention shifting back to the forest around them.

"We hold position," she said.

Richard nodded.

"Alright."

The group settled.

Not resting.

Not relaxing.

But waiting.

Lydia moved slowly along the ridge, her gaze shifting between the terrain, the canopy, the direction of the wind, the angle of the slope.

She was no longer comparing the forest to the map.

She was comparing the forest to itself.

Dooley watched her for a moment.

Then spoke quietly.

"She's figuring it out."

Ashton nodded.

"Yes."

Milo added softly.

"She has to."

Richard stood still, his eyes moving across the trees, the ground, the subtle shifts that defined this place.

The forest was no longer something they were passing through.

It was something they were inside.

And it was changing.

Not against them.

But without regard for them.

Lydia stopped.

She turned.

And nodded once.

"I know where we are."

That was enough.

Richard met her gaze.

"Then we move."

The group reformed.

Closer now.

More aware.

They stepped forward again.

Not following the map.

Not relying on markers.

But trusting—

What they were learning.

And as they moved deeper along the ridge, one thing became clear.

The forest was no longer something they could interpret from the outside.

They had to understand it—

From within.

Chapter 14 — The Mark in the Stone

The ridge leveled gradually.

Not flattening completely, but easing enough that their footing became more consistent. The ground held firm beneath them, the shifting layers from earlier giving way to a more settled structure of compact soil and embedded stone.

The wind lessened.

Not gone.

But reduced.

The forest seemed to draw back into itself again, the restless motion in the canopy settling into a more familiar rhythm.

Richard noticed the change.

"Soil's holding," he said quietly.

Ashton nodded. "Stability's improved."

Dooley glanced down at his footing. "I am a fan of stability."

Milo's attention moved ahead.

"The trees are changing again," he said.

Richard followed his gaze.

They were.

Not in height.

But in spacing.

The trunks stood slightly farther apart, their roots less tangled at the surface. The undergrowth thinned in patches, creating narrow lines of visibility that hadn't been present deeper within the forest.

It wasn't open.

But it was… clearer.

Lydia slowed.

Then stopped.

The others followed immediately.

She didn't move forward.

Didn't speak.

Her gaze had fixed on something ahead.

Richard stepped beside her.

At first, he saw only stone.

A low rise of it, partially embedded in the ground, worn smooth by time and growth.

Then—

He saw the mark.

Not natural.

A line.

Then another.

Intersecting.

Cut into the surface of the stone with deliberate intent.

Ashton moved closer, brushing away a thin layer of dirt and moss.

The pattern emerged.

Simple.

Angular.

Two lines crossing, with a third etched slightly above.

Dooley leaned in.

"That's not erosion."

"No," Ashton said. "It's cut."

Milo crouched slightly, studying the edges.

"Not recent," he said.

Lydia stepped forward slowly.

Her expression had changed.

Not surprise.

Recognition.

She knelt beside the stone, her hand hovering just above the marking.

"This is not tribal," she said quietly.

Richard looked at her. "You're sure?"

"Yes."

She traced the air just above the lines.

"The tribes do not mark stone like this," she said. "Their symbols are curved. Flowing. These—" she gestured lightly, "—are direct. Functional."

Ashton looked at the pattern again.

"Directional?" she asked.

Lydia nodded once.

"Yes."

Dooley blinked. "Directional as in… pointing somewhere?"

Lydia looked at him.

"Yes."

That shifted everything.

Richard stepped closer.

"This could be his," he said.

"The thief."

Lydia didn't answer immediately.

She studied the marking again.

Longer this time.

Then—

"No," she said.

Dooley frowned. "But it looks like something he would do."

"Yes," Lydia said. "But it is too precise."

She looked up.

"Too consistent."

Ashton straightened slightly. "Meaning?"

"Meaning this is not the first mark," Lydia said.

The forest seemed to grow quieter again.

Not in sound.

But in attention.

Milo looked around slowly.

"Someone else has been here," he said.

Serana stepped forward, her posture shifting subtly.

"Recently?" she asked.

Lydia shook her head.

"Not recently," she said. "But not ancient either."

She rose slowly.

Her gaze moved outward.

Following the direction of the mark.

Richard turned with her.

At first, there was nothing obvious.

Just trees.

Growth.

The same layered complexity they had been moving through for hours.

Then—

He saw it.

A slight break.

Not a path.

Not clearly defined.

But a line where the undergrowth thinned just enough to suggest repeated passage.

Dooley followed his gaze.

"Oh," he said quietly. "That's not random."

"No," Ashton said.

"It isn't."

Richard looked at Lydia.

"This leads somewhere."

"Yes."

Her voice was steady.

But there was something beneath it now.

Something new.

Not uncertainty.

Not doubt.

Recognition of scale.

"This was not made for a single journey," she said.

Dooley blinked again.

"Meaning what?"

Lydia met his gaze.

"Meaning someone has come through here more than once."

Milo stood slowly.

"And not recently."

"No," Lydia said.

"But not so long ago that it has disappeared."

Serana's eyes moved along the line of the break.

"Then we are not the first to follow this."

Richard felt that settle.

Not as fear.

But as awareness.

The forest was not untouched.

Not completely.

There were stories here.

Paths.

Movements.

Decisions made before they arrived.

He looked back at the stone.

The mark.

Simple.

Clear.

Intentional.

"Could he have found this?" Richard asked.

Lydia considered.

"Yes," she said.

"If he did, it would have guided him."

Ashton nodded slowly. "That explains the map."

Milo added, "The parts that made sense."

Dooley looked between them.

"So the map wasn't just his memory."

"No," Lydia said.

"It was influenced."

That mattered.

A lot.

Richard stepped forward.

Looking down the faint line through the trees.

"Then this is our best lead."

Serana didn't argue.

But she didn't agree immediately either.

"Or it's a trap," she said.

Dooley nodded slowly. "That also feels possible."

Ashton folded her arms slightly. "Not a trap in the traditional sense."

"Then what?"

"An assumption," Ashton said. "Something that leads where it once mattered, but not necessarily where we need to go."

Lydia listened.

Then nodded.

"That is possible."

Richard looked at her.

"What do you think?"

She didn't answer right away.

She stepped back to the stone.

Looked at the mark again.

Then at the line through the forest.

Then at the surrounding terrain.

She was reading it.

Not the map.

Not the marking.

The forest.

After a long moment—

She turned.

"We follow it," she said.

No hesitation.

No uncertainty.

Serana nodded once.

"Then we follow carefully."

Richard gave a single nod.

"Same formation."

Ashton stepped in.

Milo adjusted position.

Dooley lifted his pack slightly.

"Following mysterious markings deeper into the forest," he said quietly. "This continues to feel like a story I would normally not volunteer for."

"No one volunteered," Ashton said.

"That is true."

Lydia stepped forward.

Into the faint line.

Serana beside her.

Richard followed.

Then the others.

Behind them, the stone remained.

The mark.

Unchanged.

Unmoving.

Ahead—

The line continued.

Faint.

Subtle.

But real.

And as they moved into it, one thing became clear.

The forest had not simply been entered.

It had been walked before.

And now—

They were walking in someone else's direction.

Chapter 15 — The Trail That Knew the Way

The line through the forest did not behave like a path.

It did not stay clear.

It did not remain consistent.

And more than once, it seemed to vanish entirely—only to reappear a few steps later as a subtle thinning of undergrowth, a shift in the angle of growth, or the faintest break in the pattern of fallen leaves.

It required attention.

Constant attention.

Lydia moved slowly at the front, her eyes no longer scanning broadly, but narrowing—focused on details that might have gone unnoticed only an hour earlier.

Serana remained just to her side, not guiding, but watching.

Richard followed closely behind.

The others stayed tight.

No one drifted now.

No one allowed space to open.

They had all felt it.

This was different.

Not just movement through the forest.

Movement along something.

Dooley kept his voice low.

"I feel like we're following a thought."

Ashton glanced at him.

"That's not entirely wrong."

"I wish it was entirely wrong."

Milo's eyes moved along the ground ahead.

"It's not a trail," he said.

"It's repetition."

That was the word.

Repetition.

Not cleared.

Not cut.

Walked.

Again and again.

Over time.

Richard stepped over a low root and paused briefly, looking ahead.

"Spacing's consistent," he said.

"Yes," Lydia replied.

"But not uniform."

She stepped slightly to the left, then back to the right, following the subtle line as it curved around a cluster of thicker growth.

"It adjusts," she said.

"To what?" Dooley asked.

"To the forest," Lydia answered.

That was the difference.

This line did not force its way through.

It moved with the land.

Around it.

Through it.

Never against it.

Serana spoke quietly.

"That's not accidental."

"No," Lydia said.

"It isn't."

They continued.

The forest grew quieter again.

Not in the same way as before.

Not the silence of a predator.

But a kind of narrowing.

Fewer distractions.

Fewer competing sounds.

As if this section of the forest held itself differently.

Richard felt it.

Not as pressure.

But as presence.

The ground beneath them changed again.

Less soil.

More stone.

Flat in places.

Uneven in others.

The roots here ran deeper, less exposed, anchoring into something more solid beneath the surface.

Ashton adjusted her footing carefully.

"This area's older," she said.

Milo nodded.

"Yes."

Dooley glanced around.

"I feel like we've entered a part of the forest that has opinions."

Ashton gave him a look.

"It always had opinions."

"This feels like stronger opinions."

Lydia didn't respond.

She had stopped.

Again.

But this time—

She didn't move forward.

Or to the side.

She looked down.

Richard stepped beside her.

"What is it?"

She pointed.

At first, he saw only stone.

Then—

He saw the edge.

A line.

Not drawn.

Not carved.

Worn.

Smooth in a way the surrounding surface was not.

Ashton crouched.

"That's been used," she said.

"Yes," Lydia replied.

She stepped forward slowly.

Following the worn line.

It curved.

Subtly.

Leading toward a cluster of stone formations just ahead.

Not large.

But distinct.

Three vertical rises.

Close together.

Like fingers pressed upward through the ground.

Dooley leaned slightly.

"Those look familiar."

Ashton brought up the map.

Her eyes moved quickly.

Then stopped.

"That's it," she said.

"The three-stone marker."

Milo stepped closer.

"That's the next point."

Richard felt it settle.

This wasn't guesswork.

This was alignment.

They had reached one of the map's true anchors.

Lydia moved carefully around the stones.

Her attention sharpened again.

Not satisfied with finding the marker.

Looking for what came after.

"This is where it changes," she said.

Dooley frowned.

"It already changed."

"It changes more here," Lydia said.

Serana's posture shifted slightly.

"Explain."

Lydia looked at the ground.

Then at the surrounding trees.

Then back at the stones.

"He didn't draw this part clearly," she said.

Ashton nodded.

"After this point, the map gets… uncertain."

Milo added quietly, "More corrections."

"Yes," Lydia said.

She stepped to one side of the stones.

Then the other.

Looking for something.

Reading.

Interpreting.

Richard waited.

Didn't rush her.

Didn't interrupt.

After a long moment—

She moved.

Not forward.

Not along the obvious continuation.

But slightly off.

To the right.

Serana followed immediately.

Richard did the same.

The others stayed close.

Dooley blinked.

"That's not the direction I would have picked."

"That's why you're not leading," Ashton said.

"That is a fair point."

They moved only a few steps.

Then Lydia stopped again.

And this time—

There was no mistaking it.

The ground dropped.

Not sharply.

Not like a cliff.

But enough.

A shallow descent.

Partially hidden by growth.

Easy to miss if you weren't looking for it.

Milo stepped closer, peering down.

"That leads somewhere."

"Yes," Lydia said.

Her voice had changed again.

Not uncertain.

But quieter.

As if something had just been confirmed.

Richard looked at her.

"This is it."

Not a question.

Lydia nodded slowly.

"This is where he left the path."

Dooley blinked.

"He left the path?"

"He stopped following what guided him," Lydia said.

"And started choosing for himself."

Ashton folded her arms slightly.

"That explains the inconsistency."

Milo looked down into the descent.

"And the mistakes."

Serana's eyes moved along the edge.

"This is where things go wrong."

Lydia didn't disagree.

"Yes."

The forest felt different here.

Not louder.

Not quieter.

Just—

Focused.

Richard stepped closer to the edge.

Looking down.

The descent curved out of sight, the lower ground obscured by thicker growth and shadow.

"This leads deeper," he said.

"Yes," Lydia replied.

Dooley shifted slightly.

"I feel like this is the part where we decide if we're continuing the story."

Ashton didn't look at him.

"We are."

Milo nodded.

"Yes."

Serana looked at Richard.

"Your call."

Richard didn't hesitate.

"We continue."

He looked at Lydia.

"You lead."

She nodded.

Once.

Then stepped forward.

Down the slope.

Serana followed.

Richard next.

Then Ashton.

Milo.

Dooley last.

The ground shifted beneath their feet as they descended.

Softer again.

Less stable.

The trees closed in slightly.

The light dimmed.

And the line they had been following—

Disappeared completely.

They were no longer on a path.

No longer guided by repetition.

Now—

They were following a choice.

One made by someone who had come before them.

And gotten this far.

Richard looked ahead.

“Stay close,” he said quietly.

The group tightened.

The forest deepened.

And somewhere ahead—

Hidden.

Waiting.

The next part of the story began.

Chapter 16 — Where the Light Fails

The descent changed everything.

Not immediately.

But steadily.

With each step downward, the forest closed in just a little more. The spacing between the trees narrowed, the canopy above thickened, and the already limited light filtered through in thinner and thinner strands until it no longer reached the ground in anything resembling clarity.

The air cooled.

The sounds shifted.

Even the ground beneath them felt different—softer in places, but with a firmness underneath that suggested stone lying just below the surface, shaping the land in ways they could not yet fully see.

Richard felt it in the way he placed his feet.

Carefully.

Deliberately.

No longer trusting that the next step would match the last.

Lydia slowed.

Then slowed further.

"We stay close," she said quietly.

No one needed the reminder.

They were already close.

Closer than before.

Serana moved just ahead now, her role shifting subtly—not leading, but ensuring that whatever lay immediately before them was read correctly before the group committed to it.

Richard remained just behind Lydia.

Ashton and Milo followed within arm's reach.

Dooley stayed tight at the rear.

No gaps.

No drift.

The forest did not allow for it anymore.

The light dimmed again.

Not because the sun had changed.

But because something above them had.

Richard glanced upward.

The canopy here was different.

Denser.

Layered in a way that blocked not just direct light, but reflected light as well. The leaves overlapped in thick formations, creating a ceiling that felt almost solid in places.

Dooley looked up too.

"Okay," he said quietly, "this is new."

Ashton nodded. "Light reduction."

"That is a very calm way of saying we're losing visibility."

Milo's voice came softer.

"It's not just darker."

Richard looked at him. "What do you mean?"

Milo gestured slightly.

"The color," he said.

Richard saw it then.

The forest here wasn't just dim.

It was muted.

The greens deeper.

The shadows thicker.

Even the movement of the air seemed less visible, as if the space itself absorbed more than it reflected.

Lydia spoke.

"This is lower growth."

She stepped forward carefully.

"Less exposure. More containment."

Dooley frowned slightly.

"That sounds like we're inside something."

Lydia didn't respond.

Not because she disagreed.

Because she didn't want to define it that way.

Serana stopped.

The group halted immediately.

"What is it?" Richard asked.

Serana didn't answer right away.

She crouched slightly, her hand hovering just above the ground.

Then—

She shifted her position.

Looking not at the surface.

But across it.

"There's a pattern here," she said.

Ashton stepped closer.

"What kind of pattern?"

Serana gestured slightly.

"Subtle," she said. "But consistent."

Richard moved in.

At first, he saw nothing unusual.

Then—

He adjusted his angle.

And the ground changed.

Not physically.

Visually.

A faint series of lines.

Not carved.

Not marked.

But formed.

In the way the soil had settled.

In the way the leaves had gathered.

In the way the smallest fragments had been pushed and shifted over time.

A direction.

Milo nodded slowly.

"Water," he said.

Lydia looked at him.

"Yes."

She stepped forward.

Her gaze moved outward, following the faint pattern.

"This area channels runoff," she said. "When it rains, water moves through here."

Dooley blinked.

"So we're standing in a path that only exists when it rains."

"Yes," Lydia said.

"That is… very specific."

"It also explains the ground," Ashton added. "Soft above, firm below."

Richard followed the direction of the pattern.

It curved.

Subtly.

Not straight.

Never straight.

But consistent.

"This leads somewhere," he said.

Lydia nodded.

"Yes."

Serana stood.

"Then we follow it."

No one argued.

The path—if it could be called that—was more difficult than anything they had followed before.

It did not remain visible.

It appeared.

Then faded.

Then appeared again.

The only way to stay on it was to understand what it represented, not what it looked like.

Water.

Flow.

Movement shaped by terrain.

Lydia led.

But now—

Milo walked beside her.

Not replacing her.

Supporting her.

Seeing things from a different angle.

"That way," he said quietly at one point, indicating a subtle shift in the slope.

Lydia adjusted immediately.

"Yes."

Ashton followed closely, confirming alignment where she could, her eyes moving between the terrain and the limited reference points they still carried.

Dooley stayed silent.

For once.

Richard noticed.

That alone said enough.

The forest grew quieter.

Not empty.

But contained.

The layered sounds from before—birds, movement in the branches, distant calls—had diminished again.

Not vanished.

But pulled back.

As if this area was not meant for constant motion.

Serana slowed.

Then stopped.

The group followed.

She listened.

Longer this time.

Then turned slightly.

"We're close to something," she said.

Richard felt it.

Not as a sound.

Not as movement.

But as—

Change.

The air shifted.

Cooler still.

And—

Damp.

Dooley noticed it next.

"Okay," he said quietly, "that smells different."

Ashton nodded. "Moisture increase."

Milo looked ahead.

"There," he said.

Richard followed his gaze.

At first—

Nothing.

Then—

Something darker.

Not shadow.

Depth.

The ground ahead dipped again.

But not like before.

This was different.

More defined.

More contained.

Lydia stepped forward slowly.

Serana beside her.

The others followed.

The descent was short.

But deliberate.

And at the base—

The forest opened.

Not wide.

Not exposed.

But enough.

Stone.

Not scattered.

Formed.

A natural rise of it, curving inward, creating a shallow wall that seemed to hold the space together.

And within that—

An opening.

Not large.

Not obvious.

But unmistakable.

Dooley stopped.

"That," he said quietly, "looks important."

Ashton nodded slowly. "Very."

Milo didn't speak.

His eyes remained fixed on the opening.

Lydia stepped closer.

Her breathing had changed.

Not faster.

Just—

Aware.

She studied the formation carefully.

The shape of the stone.

The angle of the opening.

The way the surrounding ground settled toward it.

"This is natural," she said.

Then—

After a pause—

"Mostly."

Serana's eyes narrowed slightly.

"Explain."

Lydia moved closer to the edge of the opening.

Not entering.

Not yet.

She gestured to the stone.

"The formation is natural," she said. "But the clearing around it…"

She shook her head slightly.

"Something has moved here."

Richard stepped beside her.

Looking into the opening.

Dark.

Not completely.

But enough that it concealed what lay beyond.

"This could be it," he said.

Lydia nodded slowly.

"Yes."

Dooley exhaled.

"So this is the cave."

Ashton glanced at him.

"Possibly."

"That's not the same as definitely."

"No," she said. "It isn't."

Milo spoke quietly.

"It matches the map."

Richard nodded.

"It does."

Serana stepped forward slightly.

Her attention sharpened.

"Then we don't rush this."

No one disagreed.

The forest held still around them.

Not silent.

But watching.

Waiting.

Richard looked at the opening again.

Then at Lydia.

"What do you think?"

She didn't answer immediately.

She looked at the cave.

Then at the ground around it.

Then at the forest beyond.

She was reading everything.

Not just the destination.

But what it meant to reach it.

After a long moment—

She nodded.

"We found it."

The words were quiet.

But certain.

And for the first time since entering the forest—

They were no longer searching.

They were there.

Richard exhaled slowly.

"Alright," he said.

"Carefully."

Serana stepped forward.

"I go first."

Lydia didn't argue.

Richard nodded.

"Together," he said.

The group tightened.

Closer than before.

More aware than ever.

And as they stepped toward the opening—

The forest behind them faded into shadow.

And the unknown—

Opened in front of them.

Chapter 17 — Into the Hollow

The opening was smaller up close.

Not so small that it forced them to crawl.

But narrow enough that the light from the forest did not travel far inside. The stone curved inward just beyond the entrance, bending the passage slightly to one side so that whatever lay deeper within was hidden almost immediately.

Serana stepped forward first.

She paused at the threshold.

Not hesitating.

Assessing.

Her hand moved lightly along the stone at the edge, not touching fully, but close enough to read the surface. Her eyes adjusted to the shift in light, narrowing slightly as she leaned just enough to see around the first curve.

She listened.

For longer than seemed necessary.

Then—

"It's clear," she said.

Not certainty.

But enough.

Lydia stepped in beside her.

Richard followed immediately behind.

The others stayed close.

The moment they crossed the threshold, the forest changed.

Not behind them.

Within them.

The sounds that had surrounded them—the layered movement, the quiet rhythm of life—faded quickly, replaced by something else.

Stillness.

Not empty.

But contained.

The air cooled further.

The scent shifted.

Less earth.

More stone.

Damp, but not wet.

Old.

That was the word Richard felt settle in his mind.

Old.

The passage curved gently inward, the walls smooth in some places, rough in others, shaped by time and slow movement rather than deliberate construction. The ceiling rose just enough to allow them to stand fully, though the space felt close regardless.

Light followed them only a short distance.

Beyond that—

Shadow.

Ashton activated a low-output light from her pack.

Not bright.

Not intrusive.

Just enough to reveal the immediate space ahead.

The beam spread softly across the stone, revealing textures and edges that would have remained hidden otherwise.

Dooley glanced back once.

The entrance was still visible.

A pale shape behind them.

Smaller already.

"That closed in quickly," he said quietly.

"It will," Lydia replied.

Her voice carried differently here.

Not louder.

But more contained.

The cave held sound.

Didn't let it travel far.

Serana moved forward again.

Each step placed with the same care she had shown outside, though her pace adjusted slightly to account for the tighter space.

Richard followed.

The others stayed within reach.

No one allowed distance to open.

The passage narrowed.

Then widened.

Then narrowed again.

Not in a predictable way.

The stone seemed to shape itself around natural pressures, forming a path that felt less like a tunnel and more like a space that had slowly made room for movement over time.

Milo ran his hand lightly along the wall.

"Water," he said.

Richard glanced at him.

"Past or present?"

"Both," Milo said.

Lydia nodded.

"This would have been part of a flow system once," she said. "Long ago."

Dooley looked at the ceiling.

"I'm glad it's not flowing now."

Ashton adjusted the light slightly.

"Still could be, depending on weather."

"That is also not comforting."

They continued.

The air shifted again.

Cooler.

Dampened further.

The light from Ashton's device revealed more of the passage ahead—and something else.

Marks.

Not obvious at first.

But present.

Scratches along the wall.

Not natural.

Too straight.

Too repeated.

Richard slowed.

"You see that?" he asked.

Ashton moved the light.

The marks became clearer.

Thin lines.

Parallel in places.

Crossing in others.

Dooley frowned.

"That doesn't look like water."

"No," Ashton said.

"It doesn't."

Lydia stepped closer.

Her hand hovered near the surface.

"These are recent," she said.

Serana's posture shifted slightly.

"Define recent."

"Not ancient," Lydia replied.

"Within years."

Richard nodded slowly.

"The thief."

"Or someone before him," Ashton said.

Milo looked ahead.

"They go deeper."

That was the direction.

The marks didn't form a clear path.

But they were consistent enough to suggest movement.

Repeated movement.

Serana moved again.

Following them.

The group stayed tight.

The passage turned.

More sharply this time.

The light shifted with it, revealing a wider space ahead.

Not large.

But open compared to the narrow passage they had just moved through.

Serana stopped.

The group halted immediately.

Richard stepped beside her.

"What is it?"

Serana didn't answer.

She stepped forward slowly.

Then—

She knelt.

Richard followed her line of sight.

At first, he saw only the ground.

Stone.

Uneven.

Then—

He saw it.

A scuff.

Then another.

Marks where something heavy had been set down.

Dragged slightly.

Moved.

Ashton stepped in, lowering the light.

"That's not natural," she said.

"No," Richard replied.

Milo crouched beside them.

"Weight," he said.

"Something dense."

Dooley leaned in.

"Like… equipment?"

"Or the Core," Ashton said.

That settled.

The space held it.

Quietly.

He had been here.

Someone had been here.

Not guessing.

Not wandering.

They had reached this point.

Richard stood slowly.

"They made it this far."

"Yes," Lydia said.

Her voice was steady.

But softer now.

As if the distance between theory and reality had closed.

Serana looked ahead.

"Then we're close."

Richard nodded.

"Closer than we've been."

The chamber extended slightly beyond the scuffed area.

Not far.

But enough.

The walls curved inward again, forming another passage.

Darker.

Narrower.

More contained.

Lydia stepped forward.

She didn't rush.

Didn't hesitate.

She simply moved.

Serana stayed beside her.

Richard followed.

The others closed in.

The air changed again.

More still.

More contained.

And—

Something else.

Dooley noticed it first.

"Okay," he said quietly, "that's new."

Ashton glanced at him.

"What?"

He pointed slightly.

"Listen."

They did.

At first—

Nothing.

Then—

A sound.

Faint.

Almost too soft to notice.

A low, irregular hum.

Not mechanical.

Not constant.

But present.

Richard felt it before he fully heard it.

A subtle vibration in the air.

Barely there.

But real.

Milo's eyes narrowed slightly.

"That's not the cave," he said.

"No," Ashton agreed.

"It isn't."

Lydia stopped.

Her gaze fixed forward.

Into the darkness ahead.

"It's here," she said.

No uncertainty.

No question.

Just recognition.

Serana stepped slightly ahead.

"Then we slow down."

They did.

Each step measured.

Each movement deliberate.

The light shifted again as Ashton adjusted it slightly, revealing more of the passage ahead.

The hum grew clearer.

Still faint.

But unmistakable now.

Richard felt his focus narrow.

Everything else fell away.

The forest.

The journey.

The uncertainty.

All of it led here.

He looked at Lydia.

She met his gaze.

A small nod.

They were ready.

Serana moved forward.

The group followed.

And just beyond the next curve—

Something waited.

Not hidden.

Not lost.

But—

Left.

Chapter 18 — What Was Left Behind

The passage curved once more.

Then opened.

Not into a large chamber.

But into a space that felt—

Defined.

As if this was the place the cave had been leading toward all along.

The walls rose slightly higher here, the ceiling uneven but stable, shaped by time and pressure into a form that held the space together without collapse. The air was still, cooler than before, and carried a faint metallic edge that did not belong to the forest.

The hum was stronger now.

Still soft.

Still irregular.

But present.

Unmistakable.

Serana stepped forward first.

Her movements slowed even further, each step placed with absolute control. Her gaze moved across the chamber—floor, walls, ceiling—checking for anything that might shift, anything that might respond to their presence.

She stopped.

Richard moved beside her.

And saw it.

At the far end of the chamber—

Resting against a natural rise of stone—

Was the Core.

It was smaller than the space around it.

And yet—

It held the room.

Encased in its reinforced housing, the Quantum StarPath Core sat partially tilted, one side resting against the stone as if it had been set down without care or simply dropped and left where it landed. The faint glow within its structure pulsed unevenly, the crystalline arrays inside shifting slowly, as though still attempting to process data long after they had been removed from the systems they were meant to serve.

Ashton lowered the light slightly.

Not to hide it.

But to let it stand on its own.

"That's it," she said quietly.

No one disagreed.

Milo stepped closer, stopping several paces away.

"It's active," he said.

"Yes," Ashton replied. "Partially."

The hum deepened slightly as if in response to their presence.

Dooley exhaled slowly.

"So they made it."

Richard nodded.

"They made it."

Lydia stood very still.

Her gaze was fixed not just on the Core—

But on the space around it.

"There's more," she said.

Serana had already seen it.

She stepped slightly to the side.

And the light shifted.

Revealing—

A shape.

On the ground.

Partially obscured by shadow.

Richard moved forward.

Carefully.

The others followed.

And the shape resolved.

A person.

Or what remained of one.

Kael Thorn.

He lay on his side, his back against the stone, one arm angled awkwardly beneath him as though he had tried to brace himself and failed. His clothing was torn in places, dirt and dust marking the fabric in uneven patterns that spoke of movement, of struggle, of time spent in conditions that offered little stability.

But it wasn't the position that held Richard's attention.

It was the stillness.

Complete.

Final.

Dooley's voice came softer than it had at any point since entering the forest.

"He didn't make it out."

No one answered.

They didn't need to.

Milo crouched slightly, not touching, just observing.

"There's no sign of injury," he said.

Ashton stepped closer, her light moving carefully across the area.

"No external trauma," she confirmed.

Serana's gaze remained sharp.

"Then what?"

Lydia stepped forward slowly.

She knelt near Kael, her expression focused, her attention moving across his position, the ground around him, the space between him and the Core.

"He was alone at the end," she said.

Richard nodded.

"Yes."

She looked at the Core.

Then back at Kael.

"He made it here," she continued.

"They brought it this far."

Her eyes moved to the scuff marks on the ground.

Then to his position.

"And then—"

She stopped.

Not because she didn't know.

Because she did.

And it mattered how she said it.

"He failed to leave," she finished.

The words settled into the chamber.

Quiet.

Unavoidable.

Dooley swallowed slightly.

"Why?"

Lydia didn't answer immediately.

She looked at the space again.

The Core.

The ground.

The passage behind them.

Then—

"The forest," she said.

Ashton frowned slightly.

"That's not specific."

"No," Lydia said.

"It isn't."

She looked at Richard.

"But it is correct."

Richard understood.

Not fully.

But enough.

He had seen it.

Felt it.

The forest didn't need to act against you.

It only needed you to misunderstand it.

Milo spoke quietly.

"He got this far," he said.

"And then he made one mistake."

"Yes," Lydia said.

"Or several small ones."

Serana stepped closer to the Core.

Her attention shifted from the body to the device.

"Is it stable?" she asked.

Ashton moved forward, her light focused now on the Core itself.

The casing showed signs of impact.

Minor.

But present.

The internal structures continued their slow rotation, though not with the smooth precision they had displayed in the briefing projection.

"It's functioning," Ashton said.

"But not correctly."

Richard stepped beside her.

"What happens if we move it?"

Ashton hesitated.

Then answered honestly.

"I don't know."

That was not ideal.

But it was real.

Dooley looked between them.

"So… we found it, but now we have to figure out how not to break it."

"That's one way to say it," Ashton replied.

Milo stood slowly.

"We can't leave it," he said.

"No," Richard agreed.

"We can't."

Lydia rose.

Her gaze returned to Kael.

"We don't leave him either," she said.

Serana nodded once.

"No."

Dooley exhaled slowly.

"That feels right."

Ashton looked at the Core again.

"Then we need a plan."

Richard stepped back slightly.

Taking in the entire chamber.

The Core.

The body.

The space.

Everything that had led to this point.

"We do this carefully," he said.

"No rushing."

"No assumptions."

Lydia met his gaze.

"Yes."

Serana added quietly.

"And no mistakes."

That was the standard now.

Higher than before.

Because now—

They were no longer searching.

They were responsible.

Richard looked at the Core one more time.

Then at Kael.

He had not come here alone.

Driven.

Desperate.

Certain that he could take something from this place and leave with it.

He had been wrong.

Richard turned back to the group.

"We move him first," he said.

"Then we assess the Core."

No one argued.

The chamber held steady around them.

The hum continued.

Soft.

Persistent.

And as they stepped forward to begin—

The reality settled fully into place.

They had found what they came for.

But the mission—

Was not over.

Not even close.

Chapter 19 — The Cost of Taking

They did not move immediately.

Even after Richard spoke.

Even after the decision had been made.

The chamber seemed to hold them in place for a moment longer, as if acknowledging what lay before them—not just the Core, not just the end of the search, but the weight of how they had arrived here.

Lydia stepped forward first.

Not toward the Core.

Toward Kael.

She knelt beside him again, more carefully this time, her movements deliberate and respectful. She did not rush. She did not reach out immediately. She simply observed, taking in the details with the same attention she had given the forest itself.

Serana stood just behind her.

Watching.

Allowing.

Richard moved closer, but kept enough distance to give Lydia space.

Ashton and Milo followed.

Dooley stayed just behind them, quieter now than he had been at any point since the mission began.

Lydia spoke softly.

"He was alone when he died," she said.

Not as a question.

As a statement.

Richard nodded. “Yes.”

She looked at Kael’s hands.

At the position of his body.

At the ground around him.

“There are no signs of struggle,” she said.

“No signs of pursuit.”

Ashton glanced at the surrounding stone. “No impact, no collapse.”

Milo added quietly, “No animal disturbance.”

Lydia nodded.

“Yes.”

She finally reached out.

Not to move him.

But to confirm what they already knew.

Her hand rested lightly near his shoulder.

Then withdrew.

“He died here,” she said.

The words settled into the chamber.

Simple.

Unavoidable.

Dooley exhaled slowly.

“That’s… not how he thought this would go.”

No one disagreed.

Richard looked at Kael again.

At the distance between him and the Core.

Not far.

But not close enough.

“They made it this far,” Richard said.

"Just not out."

Lydia stood.

She turned slowly toward the Core.

Her gaze moved between the two.

"He separated himself from it," she said.

Ashton frowned slightly. "Meaning?"

"He didn't die holding it," Lydia said.

"He set it down."

Serana's eyes narrowed slightly.

"Why?"

That was the question.

The one that mattered.

Richard stepped forward.

Carefully.

He stopped just short of the Core.

Looking down at it.

The casing showed more detail up close.

Scoring along one edge.

Minor deformation where it had impacted the stone.

The internal arrays still moved.

But unevenly.

The hum shifted slightly as he approached.

Not louder.

But more… aware.

Ashton moved beside him.

"Don't touch it yet," she said.

"I wasn't planning to."

"Good."

She crouched slightly, studying the surface.

"The housing's intact," she said. "Mostly."

"Mostly?" Dooley asked.

"Internal stability is off," Ashton replied.

She adjusted her light.

The glow within the Core pulsed.

Irregular.

"Something's not right," she said.

Milo stepped closer.

"It's still working," he said.

"Yes," Ashton replied.

"But not correctly."

Richard looked at her.

"What does that mean?"

Ashton hesitated.

Then answered carefully.

"It means it's trying to do something it can't complete."

That wasn't good.

Lydia stepped forward slowly.

Her gaze fixed on the Core.

"Is it responding to the environment?" she asked.

Ashton nodded slightly.

"Possibly."

Serana's voice came low.

"Or reacting to damage."

"Or both," Ashton said.

Dooley shifted slightly.

"So… we're standing next to a broken piece of advanced technology that might still be doing something we don't understand."

Ashton glanced at him.

"That's accurate."

"I would like that to be less accurate."

Richard didn't respond.

His attention had shifted.

To the ground.

Between Kael and the Core.

There.

Something subtle.

A pattern in the dust.

He crouched slightly.

"What is it?" Milo asked.

Richard pointed.

Marks.

Faint.

But present.

Not from dragging.

Not from movement.

From hesitation.

As if Kael had approached the Core.

Then stepped back.

Then forward again.

Then back.

Ashton saw it.

"He didn't just set it down," she said.

"No," Richard replied.

"He hesitated."

Lydia looked at the pattern.

Then at the Core.

Then back at Kael.

"He didn't understand what it was doing," she said.

Serana nodded.

"And he reacted too late."

Dooley frowned.

"Too late for what?"

No one answered immediately.

Because the answer was not clear.

And that was the problem.

The chamber held its quiet.

But something had changed.

Not in the air.

Not in the light.

In their understanding.

They were no longer just retrieving an object.

They were dealing with something active.

Something unresolved.

Ashton stood slowly.

"We need to stabilize it before we move it," she said.

Richard nodded.

"How?"

Ashton exhaled slightly.

"That's the part I'm working on."

Milo glanced at the Core again.

"It's reacting to something," he said.

"Yes," Ashton replied.

"The question is what."

Lydia stepped back slightly.

Giving the Core space.

"The forest?" she asked.

Ashton considered.

"Possible," she said.

"But not likely in a direct way."

Serana's gaze moved around the chamber.

"Then what?"

Ashton looked at the Core again.

Longer this time.

Then—

She saw it.

Her expression shifted.

Subtle.

But clear.

"What?" Richard asked.

Ashton stepped slightly to the side.

Adjusting the angle of her light.

"Look at the alignment," she said.

Richard followed her gaze.

The Core wasn't just resting against the stone.

It was—

Tilted.

Not randomly.

Not from impact alone.

It had settled at an angle.

Specific enough to matter.

Milo saw it next.

"It's trying to compensate," he said.

"Yes," Ashton replied.

"For what?"

Ashton didn't answer immediately.

She moved closer.

Carefully.

Not touching.

Just observing.

Then—

"For positioning," she said.

"It's trying to orient itself."

Richard frowned.

"Without a ship?"

"Yes."

Dooley blinked.

"That seems like a problem."

"It is," Ashton said.

Serana's voice came low.

"And if we move it?"

Ashton looked at her.

"Then we change whatever it's trying to do."

Silence followed.

Heavy.

Measured.

Richard stood.

Looking between the Core and Kael.

"He didn't just run out of time," he said.

"He didn't know how to handle it."

Lydia nodded.

"Yes."

Milo added quietly.

"And it didn't stop."

That was it.

The Core hadn't failed.

It had continued.

Trying to do its job.

Without the system it needed.

Without context.

Without control.

Richard exhaled slowly.

"Then we do this differently."

Ashton looked at him.

"How?"

He met her gaze.

"We don't rush it."

Serana nodded once.

"Agreed."

Lydia stepped forward slightly.

Her voice steady.

"We understand it first."

Dooley gave a small, careful nod.

"That feels like the correct approach."

Richard looked at each of them.

"Alright," he said.

"We stabilize it."

"Then we move him."

"And then we get out."

No one argued.

Because now—

They understood something Kael Thorn had not.

Taking something from this place—

Was not the same as leaving with it.

And the cost of that misunderstanding—

Still lay on the ground beside them.

Chapter 20 — Bringing It Back to Stillness

No one moved for a moment after the plan was spoken.

Not because they didn't understand what needed to be done.

But because they did.

The Core was not broken.

Not completely.

It was trying to function.

And that was the problem.

Ashton stepped forward first.

Slowly.

Carefully.

She lowered herself to one knee beside the device, her light angled so it revealed the outer casing without flooding the chamber in brightness.

"Don't crowd it," she said quietly.

The others stepped back just enough to give her space.

Not far.

But clear.

Richard watched her hands.

Not touching yet.

Reading.

Her eyes moved across the surface, following the lines of the housing, the subtle distortions from impact, the alignment against the stone.

"It's compensating for orientation drift," she said.

Milo moved closer to her side.

"How far off?" he asked.

Ashton tilted her head slightly.

"Enough to matter," she said.

"That's not helpful."

"It's accurate."

Lydia stepped forward.

Not interfering.

Observing.

"What should it be aligned to?" she asked.

Ashton hesitated.

Then answered.

"Originally? A ship's navigation grid. External references. Deep-space anchors."

She looked at the Core again.

"It doesn't have any of that now."

Serana's voice came low.

"Then what is it using?"

Ashton glanced up.

"Whatever it can find."

That wasn't reassuring.

Richard stepped closer.

"What does that mean for us?"

Ashton looked at him.

"It means it's trying to solve a problem without enough information."

Milo nodded slowly.

"So it keeps trying."

"Yes."

"And failing."

"Yes."

The hum shifted again.

Slightly stronger.

Then uneven.

Dooley leaned back instinctively.

"Okay, that sounds less stable."

Ashton didn't disagree.

"No," she said.

"It doesn't."

Lydia looked at the Core.

Then at the chamber.

Then at the ground beneath it.

Her expression changed.

Subtle.

But focused.

"It's not just misaligned," she said.

Ashton glanced at her.

"What do you mean?"

Lydia stepped closer.

Carefully.

She moved to the opposite side of the Core, her gaze shifting between its position and the surrounding stone.

"It's responding to this place," she said.

Ashton frowned slightly.

"Explain."

Lydia gestured lightly to the chamber.

"The ground slopes here," she said. "The walls curve inward. The space directs movement."

She looked back at the Core.

"It's trying to interpret this as a reference."

Milo's eyes narrowed slightly.

"Like a map."

"Yes," Lydia said.

"But it's the wrong kind of map."

That landed.

Ashton leaned back slightly.

"Environmental interference," she said.

"Exactly."

Richard stepped in.

"So we remove the interference."

Ashton nodded.

"Yes."

Serana's gaze sharpened.

"How?"

Ashton looked at the Core.

Then at the ground.

Then back at the Core.

"We level it," she said.

Dooley blinked.

"That's it?"

"That's the first step."

Milo nodded.

"If it's trying to orient, we give it a neutral baseline."

"Yes," Ashton said.

Lydia looked at the stone beneath the Core.

"This surface isn't stable," she said.

"No," Ashton agreed.

"It isn't."

Richard stepped closer.

"Then we make it stable."

Serana nodded once.

"Carefully."

They moved as a unit.

No rush.

No wasted motion.

Milo gathered small, flat stones from the edges of the chamber—pieces that had broken naturally from the surrounding rock. Ashton directed where to place them, her eye for balance and alignment guiding the process.

"Here," she said. "And there. Keep it even."

Dooley crouched beside him, passing stones one at a time.

"I feel like we are doing something very simple," he said quietly.

"We are," Ashton replied.

"And also very important."

"That too."

Lydia watched the structure form.

Not intervening.

But ready.

Serana remained just behind them, her attention never leaving the space around the group.

Richard positioned himself opposite Ashton.

"On your signal," he said.

Ashton nodded.

"Not yet."

She adjusted one of the stones.

Then another.

Then stepped back.

"Now," she said.

"Slow."

Richard and Milo moved first.

Hands placed carefully on the sides of the Core.

Not gripping.

Supporting.

Dooley hesitated for half a second—

Then stepped in.

"Okay," he said quietly. "We are doing this."

"Lift," Ashton said.

They raised it.

Only slightly.

Just enough.

The weight was immediate.

Dense.

More than expected.

Milo adjusted his stance.

"Careful," he said.

"I've got it," Richard replied.

They held.

Ashton slid the final support stone into place.

"Lower," she said.

They did.

Slowly.

The Core settled onto the makeshift base.

The hum changed.

Not louder.

Not quieter.

Different.

Ashton leaned in.

Watching.

Waiting.

For a moment—

Nothing happened.

Then—

The internal arrays shifted.

More smoothly.

The uneven pulse began to stabilize.

Not perfect.

But better.

Milo exhaled slightly.

"That helped."

"Yes," Ashton said.

"But it's not enough."

Of course it wasn't.

Richard stepped back.

"What else?"

Ashton looked at the Core again.

Longer.

Then—

"It still doesn't have a reference," she said.

Lydia stepped forward.

Her gaze moved across the chamber.

Then to the entrance behind them.

Then back to the Core.

"What does it need?" she asked.

Ashton answered carefully.

"Direction," she said.

"Relative position."

Lydia nodded slowly.

Then—

She turned.

Looking toward the passage they had come through.

"Out there," she said quietly.

"The forest is consistent."

Ashton frowned slightly.

"In what way?"

Lydia met her gaze.

"It doesn't try to define itself," she said.

"It simply is."

Milo's eyes widened slightly.

"A neutral reference," he said.

"Yes," Lydia replied.

Ashton understood.

"You want to orient it to the entrance."

"Yes."

Richard stepped forward.

"That could work."

Serana's voice came low.

"Or it could make it worse."

Ashton nodded.

"That's the risk."

Richard looked at her.

"What do you need?"

Ashton met his gaze.

"We turn it," she said.

"Just enough."

The group repositioned.

More carefully this time.

No wasted movement.

No hesitation.

Richard and Milo took primary support again.

Dooley assisted.

Ashton guided.

Lydia watched the alignment.

Serana watched everything else.

"Slow," Ashton said.

They lifted.

Again.

The weight no lighter.

But more controlled now.

"Rotate," Ashton said.

"Two degrees."

Richard adjusted.

Milo matched.

Dooley held steady.

"Stop."

They held.

Ashton checked the alignment.

Then nodded.

"Lower."

They did.

The Core settled.

The hum—

Changed.

This time—

It stabilized.

Not completely.

But enough.

The internal arrays began to move with a smoother rhythm, the erratic pulses evening out into something closer to what they had seen in the briefing.

Ashton leaned in.

Watching.

Waiting.

Then—

She nodded.

"That's it."

Milo exhaled.

"It's holding."

Dooley leaned back slightly.

"I like when things hold."

Serana stepped forward.

"Is it safe to move?"

Ashton hesitated.

Then—

"Yes," she said.

"Carefully."

Richard looked at Lydia.

She met his gaze.

A small nod.

They had done it.

Not perfectly.

But correctly.

Richard straightened.

"Alright," he said.

"We move him."

The chamber felt different now.

Not safer.

But resolved.

The Core no longer struggled against itself.

It had been brought—

Not to full function.

But to stillness.

And that—

Was enough.

For now.

Richard looked once more at Kael Thorn.

Not alone in how he had come here.

But alone in how it had ended.

Then at the Core.

“Let’s finish this,” he said.

The group moved.

Together.

And for the first time since entering the cave—

They were no longer reacting.

They were acting.

And that made all the difference.

Chapter 21 — The Way Back Is Not the Same

They moved Kael first.

Carefully.

With purpose.

There was no rush in the way they lifted him—no urgency that would reduce the moment to a task.

Ashton unfolded a compact field blanket from her pack—thin, metallic, reflective.

She hesitated only a moment, then nodded.

"Let's wrap him," she said quietly.

Dooley moved to assist.

Together they drew the material around Kael's body, securing it without tightening—protective, not restrictive. The surface caught the dim cave light, soft reflections shifting as they worked.

Richard and Milo took the primary weight, adjusting their grip so that his body remained supported without strain.

Lydia stepped back slightly.

Not distant.

But giving space.

Serana watched the chamber.

Always watching.

"Slow," Richard said.

They lifted.

The weight was less than expected.

Not because it was light.

Because it was still.

That made it harder.

They adjusted.

Stabilized.

Then began to move.

Behind them, the Core remained where it had been stabilized.

Not abandoned.

Not forgotten.

Waiting.

Lydia glanced back once.

"It will hold," she said.

"For now," Ashton added.

Richard gave a small nod.

"We come back for it."

No one questioned that.

The passage behind them waited.

There was no rush in the way they lifted him—no urgency that would reduce the moment to a task. Richard and Milo took the primary weight, adjusting their grip so that his body remained supported without strain. Ashton guided positioning. Dooley assisted where needed, quieter than he had been since the mission began.

Lydia stepped back slightly.

Not distant.

But giving space.

Serana watched the chamber.

Always watching.

"Slow," Richard said.

They lifted.

The weight was less than expected.

Not because it was light.

Because it was still.

That made it harder.

They adjusted.

Stabilized.

Then began to move.

Behind them, the Core remained where it had been stabilized.

Not abandoned.

Not forgotten.

Waiting.

Lydia glanced back once.

"It will hold," she said.

"For now," Ashton added.

Richard gave a small nod.

"We come back for it."

No one questioned that.

The passage behind them waited.

Narrow.

Curving.

Less familiar now that they were leaving with more than they had brought in.

Ashton dimmed the light slightly.

"Keep it low," she said. "No sudden changes."

Milo nodded.

"Watch the footing."

Dooley exhaled softly.

"I am very aware of my footing."

Serana moved ahead.

Clearing the path.

Reading each turn before the group reached it.

"Step here," she said quietly.

They followed.

No deviation.

No hesitation.

The chamber fell behind them.

The Core remained where it had been stabilized—ready to be moved next.

But not yet.

Not until Kael was clear.

The passage felt tighter on the way out.

Not physically.

But perceptually.

The walls seemed closer.

The turns sharper.

The light less certain.

Richard felt it in the way he moved.

Every step required more attention.

Every shift in weight had to be controlled.

Behind him, Ashton guided.

"Careful—low rise," she said.

Milo adjusted.

Richard followed.

Dooley stayed close.

No one spoke more than necessary.

The cave held sound differently now.

Their movement echoed.

Softly.

But enough to remind them that they were no longer just passing through.

They were carrying something out.

The first curve passed.

Then the second.

The faint light from the entrance appeared.

Small.

Distant.

But real.

Dooley saw it first.

"There," he said quietly.

"Good," Ashton replied.

"Very good."

Lydia remained focused.

Her attention had shifted again.

Not just on the path.

On the transition.

The moment they would leave the cave and re-enter the forest.

"That's where it changes," she said softly.

Richard heard her.

Understood.

The cave had been contained.

The forest would not be.

They reached the threshold.

The light expanded.

Not bright.

But enough.

Serana stepped out first.

Paused.

Listened.

Then—

"Clear," she said.

They followed.

Carefully.

One step at a time.

Out of the cave.

Back into the forest.

The air had changed.

Immediately.

The moment they crossed the threshold.

Cooler.

More active.

The stillness of the cave replaced by movement—subtle, but constant.

Richard felt it in the shift of wind through the trees.

Stronger than before.

Less controlled.

Dooley noticed it next.

"Okay," he said quietly, "that's different."

Ashton nodded.

"Storm system moved in."

Milo looked upward.

What little of the canopy they could see shifted more aggressively now, the leaves moving in uneven waves as the wind pushed through the upper layers.

Lydia stepped forward.

Her gaze moved quickly across the surrounding terrain.

"The ground will change," she said.

Serana nodded.

"It already has."

Richard adjusted his stance.

"We don't linger," he said.

"No," Lydia agreed.

"We don't."

They moved.

The path they had taken in no longer existed.

Not in the way it had before.

The subtle patterns, the faint lines of movement, the environmental cues they had relied on—

Were disrupted.

Shifted.

Altered by the changing conditions.

Ashton activated the map briefly.

Then lowered it.

"It won't help much now," she said.

Milo nodded.

"We follow the terrain."

"Yes," Lydia said.

"Not the memory."

That was the difference.

Dooley glanced back once.

The cave was already less visible.

The entrance blending into the surrounding stone and growth as if it had never been distinct to begin with.

"I don't like how fast that disappears," he said.

"That's the forest," Lydia replied.

"It doesn't preserve your path."

Serana moved ahead.

"Stay close," she said.

They did.

The wind increased.

Not violent.

But persistent.

It moved through the trees with uneven force, causing branches to shift, leaves to fall, and the ground to respond in subtle ways that made footing less predictable.

Richard felt it immediately.

The soil beneath them softened in places, compacted in others.

The balance they had relied on before—

Was no longer consistent.

"Watch your step," Ashton said.

Milo adjusted.

"Ground's shifting again."

Dooley nodded.

"I am beginning to understand why this place is not open to visitors."

Lydia moved carefully.

Her attention sharper now.

Not just reading the forest.

Anticipating it.

"The ridge," she said.

Richard followed her gaze.

It was there.

Faint.

But present.

Higher ground.

More stable.

"Same plan?" he asked.

"Yes," Lydia replied.

Serana nodded.

"Move."

They adjusted course.

Slowly.

Deliberately.

Carrying Kael.

The added weight changed everything.

Their pace slowed.

Their balance required more attention.

Their margin for error narrowed.

But they held formation.

No one drifted.

No one rushed.

Dooley kept his voice low.

"I would like to note that carrying someone through a shifting forest is not easy."

"No," Ashton said.

"It isn't."

"But we are doing it."

"Yes," she said.

"We are."

Richard glanced ahead.

The ridge approached.

Closer now.

More defined.

"We get there," he said, "we reassess."

Lydia nodded.

"Yes."

Serana moved first.

Testing.

Each step confirmed before the next.

They reached the ridge.

And the ground—

Held.

Better.

Not perfect.

But better.

Milo exhaled slightly.

"Stable enough."

Ashton nodded.

"For now."

Richard adjusted his grip.

"Set him down."

They did.

Carefully.

Gently.

Not dropping.

Not releasing.

Placing.

Lydia stepped closer.

Her gaze moved across Kael again.

Then outward.

Toward the forest.

"The way back is not the same," she said.

Richard nodded.

"No."

Serana added quietly.

"And it won't become easier."

That was understood.

They had entered the forest under one set of conditions.

They would leave under another.

Different.

Unpredictable.

Unforgiving.

Richard stood.

Looking at each of them.

"We've done the hard part," he said.

Ashton shook her head slightly.

"No," she said.

"We've done the precise part."

Milo added quietly.

"Now we do the difficult part."

Dooley exhaled.

"I was hoping those were the same."

"They're not," Ashton said.

Richard looked at Lydia.

"What's next?"

She held his gaze for a moment.

Then—

"We're not finished," she said.

Ashton understood immediately.

"The Core."

No one argued.

They didn't need to.

The return to the cave was quieter.

Not because the forest had settled.

Because they had.

They moved with less uncertainty now.
Not faster.

But clearer.

Serana led.

Lydia followed close behind.

The entrance revealed itself only at the last moment—
as if the forest allowed it,
but did not offer it.

They entered.

The chamber had not changed.

The Core remained where they had left it.

Still.

But not at rest.

Ashton studied it from a distance.

"Not stable," she said.
"Not fully."

Richard nodded.
"What does it need?"

She glanced toward the entrance.
"Light," she said.
"Or something close to it."

Dooley tilted his head slightly.
"That seems… important."

"It is," Ashton replied.

They did not rush.

Dooley and Milo adjusted their grip.

Richard stepped in.

Together, they lifted the Core.

It resisted—not physically, but in the way it held itself.

Not wanting to move.

But not stopping them.

They carried it carefully.

Out of the chamber.

Through the passage.

Toward the entrance.

The moment it crossed into the open air—

Something changed.

Not dramatically.

Not visibly at first.

But the tension—

Released.

The surface of the Core shifted slightly, its structure settling into alignment.

Ashton stepped closer.

"Wait," she said.

They held position.

No one moved.

Seconds passed.

Then—

"It's stabilizing," she said quietly.

Richard watched her.

"You're sure?"

She nodded once.

"Yes."

She stepped forward.

Hands steady.

Movements precise.

"This should have been done earlier," she said.

Dooley glanced at her.

"By Kael?"

"Yes."

A small pause.

"He activated it in the ship," Ashton continued. "But he never completed the shutdown sequence."

Richard absorbed that.

An error.

Not careless.

But costly.

Ashton began.

Her hands moved across the surface—
not touching in the traditional sense,
but interacting.

Reading.

Responding.

The Core answered.

Not with sound.

But with alignment.

Each motion she made brought it closer to stillness.

Closer to completion.

Then—

She stopped.

The Core went quiet.

Not inactive.

But at rest.

"It's done," she said.

Safe.

Contained.

Transportable.

They carried it back.

More easily this time.

Not because it weighed less.

Because it resisted less.

They returned to the ridge.

Lydia looked at the Core.

Then at Ashton.

"It's stable?"

"Yes."

A small nod.

"Good."

Richard looked at the group.

Then again—

"What's next?"

She met his gaze.

"We go back," she said.

"But not the way we came."

That was the truth.

Clear.

Unavoidable.

The forest had shifted.

The path had changed.

And now—

They would have to earn their way out.

Richard nodded once.

"Alright," he said.

"Then we move."

They lifted again.

Reformed.

Tight.

Focused.

And as they stepped forward—

Away from the cave—

The wind carried through the trees.

The forest moved around them.

And the journey—

Turned toward home.

Chapter 22 — When Direction Disappears

The ridge did not hold as long as Richard had hoped.

It carried them forward for a time—long enough to regain rhythm, long enough to establish footing, long enough to feel, briefly, that the return might follow a pattern they could understand.

Then—

It curved.

And in that curve—

It disappeared.

Not abruptly.

Not like a break.

But gradually enough that, by the time Richard realized the ground beneath them had changed, they were no longer on it.

The soil softened again.

The roots returned.

The subtle instability beneath the surface followed.

Milo noticed first.

"Ground's shifting," he said quietly.

Ashton nodded. "We've left the ridge."

Dooley glanced down.

"I liked the ridge."

"Yes," Ashton said. "We all did."

Lydia slowed.

Then stopped.

The group halted immediately.

No hesitation.

No questions.

Not anymore.

She turned slowly.

Not looking at the map.

Not scanning for landmarks.

Reading.

The forest.

The wind.

The ground.

Everything.

Richard watched her.

He had seen this before.

Earlier.

But now—

It was different.

She wasn't comparing what she saw to what she had studied.

She was understanding it.

In real time.

"We're off alignment," Ashton said quietly.

"Yes," Lydia replied.

"But not lost."

Dooley let out a small breath.

"That's good to hear."

Milo looked around.

"The flow changed," he said.

"The water path we followed in is gone."

Lydia nodded.

"Yes."

The ground confirmed it.

The subtle patterns of runoff they had used before had been disrupted by the shifting wind and moisture. What had once been readable now scattered into fragments that no longer connected cleanly.

Richard adjusted his grip on Kael.

"What do we use instead?"

Lydia didn't answer immediately.

She stepped forward.

Then to the side.

Then back.

Her gaze lifted.

To the canopy.

Then lowered again.

To the ground.

Then outward.

To the spacing of the trees.

She was building something.

Not from a map.

From observation.

Serana spoke quietly.

"Take your time."

Lydia nodded.

"I am."

The wind shifted again.

Stronger now.

Not enough to push them.

But enough to change how the forest moved.

Branches swayed.

Leaves fell.

The sounds layered differently.

What had once been consistent patterns of movement now broke into irregular waves.

Dooley kept his voice low.

"I feel like the forest is rearranging itself."

"It's not," Ashton said.

"It's responding."

"That sounds worse."

Milo didn't look away from the terrain.

"It's revealing what matters," he said.

Lydia stopped.

Completely.

The group followed.

She crouched slightly.

Not touching the ground.

Watching it.

"Here," she said.

Richard stepped closer.

"What is it?"

She gestured.

At first—

Nothing.

Then—

He saw it.

A slight difference.

Not in the surface.

In the density.

The soil here was packed tighter.

Not hard.

But more resistant.

Ashton noticed it next.

"Compaction," she said.

"Yes," Lydia replied.

"Movement," Milo added.

"Repeated," Lydia confirmed.

Dooley blinked.

"So… another path?"

"No," Lydia said.

"Not a path."

She stood.

"Direction."

That was the distinction.

Richard looked ahead.

The pattern extended.

Faint.

But consistent.

Not carved.

Not worn.

Pressed.

By time.

By movement.

By something that had passed through this area again and again—not in a line, but in a general direction.

Serana nodded once.

"That works."

Richard met Lydia's gaze.

"Lead."

They moved.

Not quickly.

Not slowly.

Precisely.

Each step placed where Lydia stepped.

Each movement adjusted as she adjusted.

The formation held tighter now.

Not because they were told to.

Because they knew to.

Dooley spoke softly.

"This feels different."

Ashton nodded.

"Yes."

"We're not looking for the path anymore."

"No," Ashton said.

"We're following understanding."

Dooley considered that.

"I like that less and more at the same time."

Milo gave a faint nod.

"That's correct."

The terrain shifted again.

But this time—

They were ready.

When the ground softened, they adjusted.

When the roots thickened, they slowed.

When the wind altered the movement above, they paused just long enough to reassess.

No panic.

No rushing.

No assumptions.

Richard felt it.

The difference.

They were no longer reacting to the forest.

They were moving with it.

Then—

The direction broke.

Not gradually.

Not subtly.

It simply—

Stopped.

Lydia halted.

The group froze.

The compaction beneath their feet ended abruptly, the ground ahead returning to the same uneven mix of soil and growth that offered no clear indication of movement.

Ashton frowned slightly.

"That's not helpful."

Milo scanned the area.

"It should continue."

"It doesn't," Dooley said.

"That is also not helpful."

Richard looked at Lydia.

"What do you see?"

She didn't answer right away.

She stepped forward.

Then back.

Then to the left.

Then to the right.

Testing.

Reading.

The forest shifted around them.

The wind moved.

The ground responded.

And then—

Lydia turned.

Not forward.

Not back.

Sideways.

"This way," she said.

Ashton blinked.

"That's not the direction we were moving."

"No," Lydia said.

"It isn't."

Milo's eyes narrowed slightly.

"You're compensating."

"Yes."

"For what?" Richard asked.

Lydia met his gaze.

"For the slope we didn't see."

Richard followed her line of sight.

And saw it.

Barely.

A subtle angle in the terrain.

Not enough to notice at a glance.

But enough to matter.

The ground wasn't level.

It tilted.

And the compaction they had followed—

Had aligned to it.

Dooley nodded slowly.

"That is… subtle."

"Yes," Lydia said.

"And important."

Serana stepped forward.

"Then we adjust."

They turned.

Following the corrected line.

The ground shifted again.

Then—

The compaction returned.

Faint.

But present.

Ashton let out a small breath.

"That's it."

Milo nodded.

"Yes."

Dooley smiled slightly.

"We found it again."

Richard glanced at Lydia.

"You didn't lose it."

She shook her head.

"No."

"I just had to understand it better."

That was the difference.

And it mattered.

They continued.

Stronger now.

More certain.

Not because the forest had become easier.

Because they had become better.

The wind moved around them.

The ground shifted beneath them.

The path appeared—

Then faded—

Then appeared again.

But this time—

They held it.

Not perfectly.

But correctly.

Richard adjusted his grip on Kael.

"We're making progress," he said.

Ashton nodded.

"Yes."

Milo added quietly.

"We're not guessing anymore."

Dooley exhaled.

"That is a very comforting development."

Serana's voice came low.

"Don't relax."

"No," Dooley said quickly.

"I will not relax."

Lydia didn't look back.

But her voice carried.

"Not yet."

They moved forward.

Together.

Focused.

Aware.

And for the first time since leaving the cave—

The direction held.

Not because the forest gave it to them.

But because—

They had learned how to find it.

And that—

Would carry them the rest of the way.

If they kept it.

If they didn't forget.

If they didn't rush.

Richard looked ahead.

"Stay sharp," he said quietly.

The group tightened.

The forest shifted.

And the way out—

Began to reveal itself.

Chapter 23 — What Follows and What Remembers

The direction held.

For a while.

Long enough that the rhythm of movement returned—steady, controlled, deliberate. The ground beneath them shifted less dramatically, the trees spaced slightly wider, and the oppressive weight of the deeper forest eased just enough to allow clearer movement.

Not safe.

But less uncertain.

Richard felt it first.

Then Ashton.

Then Milo.

Even Dooley noticed.

"This feels… familiar," he said quietly.

Ashton nodded.

"Yes."

"Familiar in a good way?"

"Familiar in a useful way."

Milo looked ahead.

"The terrain is opening," he said.

Lydia slowed.

Not stopping.

Just adjusting.

"Yes," she said.

"We're moving back toward an upper zone."

Serana remained alert.

Always.

But her posture shifted slightly—not relaxed, not lowered—but less compressed than it had been in the deeper sections.

Richard adjusted his grip on Kael.

"We're getting close."

Lydia didn't answer.

Not immediately.

Because close did not mean safe.

The ground sloped downward.

Subtly at first.

Then more clearly.

The soil softened again, though not in the unstable way they had encountered earlier. This was different—more consistent, more shaped by something that had moved through it repeatedly over time.

Milo noticed.

"Water again," he said.

"Yes," Lydia replied.

She looked ahead.

"The river."

Dooley exhaled.

"I liked the river."

Ashton glanced at him.

"You said that before."

"Yes," Dooley said. "And I continue to stand by it."

Richard allowed himself a small breath.

The river was a known point.

A confirmed reference.

Something that connected their movement now to their movement before.

That mattered.

They moved carefully.

The sound reached them before the sight.

Water.

Steady.

Unchanged.

The forest did not alter everything.

Some things remained.

That was one of them.

They reached the bank.

The same curve.

The same uneven edge.

The same subtle movement of current across stone.

Richard nodded once.

"This is it."

Ashton checked the map briefly.

"Confirmed."

Milo crouched slightly.

"The crossing point is upstream."

Lydia nodded.

"Yes."

Dooley looked at the water.

"I am very glad we are not guessing this part."

"We're not," Ashton said.

"Good."

They moved along the bank.

Slower now.

Not because they needed to.

Because they chose to.

The stones appeared.

Natural.

Placed by the river itself.

Unchanged.

Serana stepped forward.

Testing.

Each step confirmed.

Stable.

She reached the far side.

"Clear," she said.

Richard nodded.

"Same order."

Milo went first.

Then Ashton.

Dooley paused briefly at the edge.

"I remember this part," he said.

"Move," Ashton replied.

"I am moving."

He crossed.

Carefully.

Richard and Milo worked together to move Kael across.

Slow.

Balanced.

No missteps.

No shifting.

The stones held.

The crossing completed.

They reached the far side.

And for a moment—

It felt like progress.

Real.

Measured.

Earned.

The forest responded.

Not with change.

But with memory.

The sounds returned.

Layered.

Familiar.

The movement in the branches.

The distant calls.

The subtle shifts that marked a living system continuing without interruption.

Dooley exhaled.

"That's better."

Ashton nodded.

"Yes."

Milo looked ahead.

"The spacing is the same as before."

Lydia confirmed.

"Yes."

They were retracing something.

Not exactly.

But close enough to matter.

Richard felt it.

The connection.

The alignment.

They were moving out.

Then—

Serana stopped.

Immediately.

The group froze.

No delay.

No question.

Richard felt it before he saw it.

The shift.

The same one.

From before.

The forest quieted.

Not completely.

But enough.

Enough to matter.

Dooley didn't speak this time.

He didn't need to.

Ashton's voice came low.

"Same pattern."

Milo nodded.

"Yes."

Lydia's gaze moved slowly across the trees.

"It remembers us," she said.

Serana stepped slightly forward.

Her posture changed.

Not aggressive.

Not defensive.

Ready.

Richard adjusted his stance.

"Stay together."

No one needed the reminder.

They were already tight.

Closer than before.

Closer than necessary.

But necessary now.

A sound.

To the right.

Soft.

Measured.

Dooley swallowed.

"That's the same thing."

"Yes," Ashton said.

"It is."

Milo didn't move.

"Not closer," he said.

"Not yet."

Serana's eyes tracked the space between the trees.

"Watching," she said.

Lydia nodded.

"Yes."

The same predator.

Or one like it.

The shadowpanther.

It had not forgotten.

It had not left.

It had waited.

Richard held position.

Didn't rush.

Didn't push forward.

"What do we do?" Dooley asked quietly.

Lydia answered.

"The same as before."

Ashton nodded.

"No sudden movement."

Milo added quietly.

"No separation."

Serana stepped slightly ahead.

"Forward," she said.

They moved.

Slow.

Controlled.

Together.

The forest watched.

Again.

The sound followed.

Not closing.

Not retreating.

Keeping pace.

Dooley kept his voice low.

"I liked it better when we were not being evaluated."

"No you didn't," Ashton said.

"You just didn't know you were."

"That is also true."

The trees began to thin.

Gradually.

Subtly.

The light increased.

Not fully.

But enough.

Richard saw it.

The shift.

"We're close," he said.

Lydia didn't answer.

But she saw it too.

The forest ahead was less dense.

The spacing wider.

The boundary—

Near.

Serana continued forward.

Unchanged.

Unaffected.

The sound behind them shifted.

Once.

Then—

Faded.

Not gone.

But no longer tracking.

Milo noticed.

"It stopped," he said.

"Yes," Lydia replied.

"We're leaving its territory."

Dooley exhaled.

"I am very comfortable with that."

The boundary appeared.

Not suddenly.

But clearly.

The posts.

The line.

The shift in land.

The place where the forest ended—

And the world outside resumed.

Richard slowed.

Then stopped.

The group halted.

No one stepped across immediately.

Not yet.

They stood there.

At the edge.

Carrying what they had brought out.

Understanding what it had taken to do it.

Lydia looked at the forest.

Then at the line.

Then back at the forest.

Serana stood beside her.

Silent.

Present.

Richard looked at each of them.

"We made it," Dooley said quietly.

Ashton nodded.

"Yes."

Milo said nothing.

He didn't need to.

Richard stepped forward.

One step.

Across the line.

The others followed.

Lydia last.

Serana beside her.

The moment they crossed—

The forest changed.

Not in sound.

Not in form.

In distance.

It was no longer around them.

It was behind them.

And it remained.

Unchanged.

Unmoved.

Watching.

Lydia turned once.

Just briefly.

Then faced forward again.

Richard adjusted his grip.

"Let's finish this," he said.

They moved.

Away from the forest.

Carrying what they had found.

And what they had learned.

And behind them—

The Eldergreen Expanse stood as it always had.

Protected.

Respected.

And—

Remembering.

Chapter 24 — What Was Given Back

The transport was waiting.

Exactly where they had left it.

Unmoved.

Unchanged.

But everything else—

Was different.

The air felt lighter.

Not because the forest had changed.

But because they were no longer inside it.

Richard noticed it in the way he breathed.

In the way the tension in his shoulders eased without him realizing it had been there.

Dooley noticed it immediately.

"Oh," he said softly, "that's better."

Ashton glanced at him.

"You say that every time we survive something."

"Yes," Dooley said. "Because I appreciate survival."

Milo stood quietly for a moment longer, looking back at the forest line.

Not studying it.

Not analyzing it.

Just—

Looking.

Then he turned.

And stepped forward.

They moved as a unit.

Toward the transport.

Serana remained near Lydia.

As she had been the entire time.

Lydia walked differently now.

Not slower.

Not faster.

Just—

Changed.

Richard saw it.

Didn't comment.

Didn't need to.

Minister Halvern stepped forward as they approached.

He had not moved far from where they had left him.

But his attention sharpened immediately as he saw them return.

Then—

Shifted.

To what they carried.

To Kael.

To the weight of it.

"You found him," he said.

It wasn't a question.

"No," Richard replied.

"We brought him back."

That mattered.

Halvern inclined his head slightly.

"Yes," he said.

"You did."

His gaze moved next—

To Lydia.

She met it.

Steady.

Certain.

"We stayed within the boundaries," she said.

"We took nothing that was not ours to take."

Halvern held her gaze for a moment.

Then nodded.

"That matters," he said.

Lydia nodded once.

"Yes."

Serana said nothing.

But her posture carried agreement.

They moved Kael onto the transport first.

Carefully.

Respectfully.

Not as cargo.

Not as an object.

But as someone who had made a choice—

And paid for it.

Dooley adjusted his grip one final time.

Then stepped back.

"That feels better," he said quietly.

Ashton nodded.

"Yes."

Milo remained silent.

Watching.

Understanding.

The Core came next.

And everything slowed.

Again.

Ashton stepped forward.

Her attention fully focused.

"We do this exactly the same way," she said.

"No change."

Richard nodded.

"Understood."

Milo moved beside him.

Dooley took position.

Serana observed.

Lydia watched.

They lifted.

Carefully.

The weight was still there.

Dense.

Unforgiving.

But—

Stable.

The hum had changed.

Not gone.

But steady.

Contained.

Controlled.

Ashton guided.

"Keep it level," she said.

"Don't adjust."

They moved.

Step by step.

Out of the forest's reach.

Into the open.

The difference was immediate.

The air shifted.

The light changed.

The Core—

Responded.

Subtly.

The internal arrays adjusted.

Not struggling.

Not compensating.

Settling.

Ashton saw it.

"It's stabilizing further," she said.

Milo nodded.

"Less interference."

Lydia watched it closely.

Then looked back at the forest.

And understood.

They placed the Core into the secured cradle on the transport.

Gently.

Deliberately.

The hum steadied.

Not perfect.

But controlled.

Enough.

Ashton stepped back.

"That's as stable as it's going to get here," she said.

Richard nodded.

"Good."

The transport began to move.

Away from the boundary.

Away from the forest.

The line faded behind them.

The posts.

The shift in land.

The place where everything had changed.

And where everything had been learned.

Dooley sat back.

Exhaled.

"I am going to remember this mission," he said.

"Yes," Ashton replied.

"You should."

Milo looked forward.

Then spoke quietly.

"We did it right."

That mattered more than success.

Richard nodded.

"Yes," he said.

"We did."

The city rose ahead of them.

Terraces.

Stone.

Order.

Structure.

It felt—

Different now.

Not because it had changed.

Because they had.

Lydia watched it.

Quiet.

Thoughtful.

Serana remained beside her.

As she always had.

The audience chamber was the same.

Unchanged.

The King and Queen stood as before.

Present.

Attentive.

Waiting.

But this time—

The space felt different.

Not formal.

Not distant.

Earned.

Richard stepped forward.

"Your Majesties."

The others followed.

The King inclined his head.

"You have returned."

"Yes, sir," Richard said.

"We have."

The Queen's gaze moved to Kael.

Then to the Core.

Then back to the cadets.

"You completed the task," she said.

Richard shook his head slightly.

"We respected it," he said.

That was the difference.

The Queen held his gaze.

Then nodded.

"Yes," she said.

"You did."

Lydia stepped forward.

Not as a princess.

Not as a guide.

As someone who had crossed a line—

And come back changed.

"We stayed within the boundaries," she said.

"We did not take what was not ours."

The King looked at her.

Not as a ruler.

As a father.

"I know," he said.

Lydia held his gaze.

Then—

She nodded.

Once.

That was enough.

The chamber held stillness.

Not empty.

But complete.

The mission was done.

The Core recovered.

The cost acknowledged.

The lesson understood.

Richard looked at the Core one final time.

Then at Lydia.

Then at the King and Queen.

"We're ready to return," he said.

The King inclined his head.

"You will always be welcome here," he said.

The Queen added quietly—

"So long as you remember why."

Richard nodded.

"We will."

Later—

Outside.

The transport prepared for departure.

The sky open.

The forest distant.

But never gone.

Dooley looked back one last time.

"I think it's still watching us," he said.

Milo nodded.

"Yes."

Ashton didn't disagree.

"It always will."

Richard stood beside Lydia.

"You did well," he said.

She shook her head slightly.

"We did," she replied.

Then—

After a moment—

"I understand it now," she said.

Richard looked at her.

"What?"

She turned slightly.

Looking toward the forest.

"Why it's protected."

Richard nodded.

"Yes."

Lydia's voice softened.

"It was never about keeping people out."

She paused.

Then finished—

"It was about making sure no one forgot how to enter."

The transport lifted.

The ground fell away.

The forest remained.

Unchanged.

Unmoved.

Remembering.

And as they rose into the open sky—

The lesson stayed with them.

Clear.

Simple.

And earned.

Some things are not meant to be taken.

Only understood—
And returned.

Chapter 25 — What Remains

The return to orbit felt different.

Not because the ship moved any slower.

Not because the systems operated any differently.

But because the mission was no longer in front of them.

It was behind them.

And that changed everything.

Richard stood at the viewport as the transport aligned with the docking corridor. The curve of the planet stretched beneath them, clouds drifting slowly across the surface, the forest far below—hidden now, indistinguishable from the rest of the landscape.

But not forgotten.

Never that.

"Docking in thirty seconds," the pilot said.

Richard nodded.

He didn't turn.

He didn't need to.

Behind him, the others were already preparing.

Ashton had been reviewing system logs from the Core since they left the surface.

Milo sat quietly, watching the data without commenting.

Dooley leaned back in his seat, arms folded, looking as though he had been thinking for a long time and had not yet decided what to say about it.

Lydia and Serana were not with them.

The absence was noticeable.

Not empty.

But defined.

The docking clamps engaged with a soft, controlled vibration.

"Dock complete," the pilot said.

"Welcome back."

Richard turned.

"Let's move."

United Earth Space Command moved quickly.

But not carelessly.

That was the difference.

The moment the Core was transferred from the transport, a specialized containment team took over—careful, measured, precise. They did not rush. They did not assume. Every movement was deliberate, guided by procedures that had been refined over years of handling technology that was not fully understood.

Ashton remained with them.

Observing.

Correcting.

Clarifying when needed.

"It's stable," she said more than once.

"But treat it as if it isn't."

They did.

Kael Thorn was transferred separately.

With respect.

With recognition.

Not as a failure.

But as someone who had reached further than most—and learned too late what that required.

Dooley stood quietly as the transfer team moved him.

Then exhaled.

"I think that part matters the most," he said.

Milo nodded.

"Yes."

Ashton didn't look up from her work.

"But not the only part."

"No," Dooley agreed.

"But the part I'm thinking about."

The debrief was shorter than Richard expected.

Not because there was less to say.

But because what needed to be said—

Was already understood.

Admiral Jack Taylor stood at the front of the room.

The same as always.

Steady.

Measured.

Watching.

"You were given a retrieval assignment," he said.

Richard nodded.

"Yes, sir."

"You returned with the objective."

"Yes, sir."

The Admiral paused.

Then—

"And you returned with more than that."

Richard met his gaze.

"Yes, sir."

A brief silence followed.

Then the Admiral nodded.

"Good."

That was it.

No extended praise.

No formal commendation.

Just recognition.

And understanding.

Later—

The team gathered.

Not formally.

Not as part of a briefing.

Just—

Together.

The way they always did after something that mattered.

Dooley leaned back in his chair.

"I have decided something," he said.

Ashton didn't look up.

"That's always concerning."

"I am no longer interested in retrieving mysterious objects from protected forests."

"That's not new."

"No," Dooley said. "But now it's official."

Milo gave the faintest hint of a smile.

Richard sat across from them.

Listening.

Letting the moment settle.

They had done it.

But not in the way they expected.

And that mattered.

Richard found himself thinking about the boundary.

About Lydia.

About Serana.

They were not part of this world.

They had one of their own.

Ashton joined them.

"The Core is secure," she said.

"Stable?"

"As much as it's going to be."

Milo stepped in.

"It's not finished," he said.

"No," Ashton replied.

"It isn't."

Dooley leaned slightly forward.

"That sounds like a future problem."

Ashton nodded.

"Yes."

Dooley sighed.

"I had a feeling."

Richard looked around the room.

At the team.

At what they had done.

And what it meant.

"We didn't just bring it back," he said.

"No," Ashton replied.

"We didn't."

Milo added quietly—

"We learned how not to take it."

That was it.

Simple.

Clear.

True.

Later—

Richard stood alone.

Briefly.

Looking out at the stars.

The same stars.

Always the same.

But never quite the same again.

He thought about the forest.

The boundary.

The way it had felt to stand at the edge.

To enter.

To understand.

And to leave.

Not with something taken.

But with something learned.

He nodded to himself.

Just once.

"Next mission," he said quietly.

Behind him—

The ship moved.

The stars held.

And somewhere ahead—

Another assignment waited.

Not easier.

Not simpler.

But ready.

Just as they were.

Cadet Log — Richard Taylor

Mission Record: Eldergreen Retrieval Assignment
Status: Completed

There are missions you remember because of what you accomplish.

And there are missions you remember because of what they change.

This was the second kind.

We were sent to retrieve a device—something valuable, something important, something that did not belong where it had been taken. On paper, it was a straightforward assignment.

Locate.

Recover.

Return.

But the moment we reached the boundary, it stopped being simple.

The forest was not hostile.

It did not act against us.

It did not need to.

It required something different—something I don't think we fully understood at the beginning.

It required us to slow down.

To observe.

To accept that not everything could be solved by moving forward.

More than once, the correct decision was to stop.

More than once, the right path was the one we almost didn't take.

And more than once, the difference between success and failure came down to whether we understood what we were walking into—or assumed that we already did.

Kael Thorn made it to the objective.

That matters.

He was capable.

Determined.

Willing to go farther than most would.

But somewhere along the way, he treated the forest like a place to pass through instead of a place to understand.

And that cost him everything.

We did not succeed because we were stronger.

Or faster.

Or better prepared.

We succeeded because we learned.

Because we listened.

Because we followed guidance when we didn't have answers.

And because, when the time came, we chose not to take what wasn't ours to take.

The Core is now secure.

Stable.

Under control.

But that is not what stays with me.

What stays with me is the boundary.

Standing there.

Knowing that everything on the other side required something different from us.

And realizing that the boundary wasn't there to keep us out.

It was there to make sure we entered the right way.

That may be the most important lesson from this mission.

Not every place is meant to be crossed quickly.

Not every objective is meant to be taken.

Some things require patience.

Some require restraint.

And some require us to change before we're ready to move forward.

We brought the Core back.

We brought Kael back.

But more than that—

We brought back an understanding I don't intend to forget.

End Log.

Cadet Log — Ashton Quinn

Mission Record: Eldergreen Retrieval Assignment
Status: Completed

The primary objective was the recovery of a Quantum StarPath Core operating outside of its intended system environment.

Initial assessment: retrieval mission with environmental complications.

Final assessment: environmental integration failure combined with operator misinterpretation.

The Core itself did not fail.

That point is important.

It continued to operate within its design parameters, attempting to orient and stabilize without the necessary external references. In the absence of those references, it defaulted to environmental input.

That is where the problem began.

The Core interpreted the surrounding terrain as a positional framework.

Incorrectly.

Continuously.

And without correction.

The result was not catastrophic failure.

It was persistent misalignment.

That distinction matters.

Kael Thorn reached the objective.

He transported the Core successfully.

But based on the evidence, he did not understand the system state he was dealing with.

He attempted to manage a device that was still active—still processing—without stabilizing it first.

That error was not immediately fatal.

But it removed his margin for recovery.

We approached the situation differently.

We did not attempt to override the system.

We did not force a solution.

We reduced variables.

We established a neutral baseline.

We aligned the Core physically before attempting to move it.

That restored partial functional stability.

Not full recovery.

But enough to proceed.

The environmental conditions of the Eldergreen Expanse introduced variables that are not typically accounted for in standard retrieval protocols.

Organic terrain.

Variable ground structure.

Non-linear reference points.

Unpredictable interference.

These conditions require a different operational mindset.

Less assumption.

More observation.

Less correction.

More alignment.

That is the technical lesson.

The non-technical lesson is harder to define.

We entered the forest expecting to solve a problem.

We left understanding that not all problems are solved by applying force or speed.

Some systems—natural or otherwise—require cooperation.

Even if they are not designed to respond to us.

The Core is now secure.

Further analysis will be conducted under controlled conditions.

I expect additional complications.

But those can be managed.

The forest cannot.

That is not a limitation.

It is a parameter.

And it should be treated as such in any future operations.

End Log.

Cadet Log — Dooley Lewis

Mission Record: Eldergreen Retrieval Assignment
Status: Completed (and survived)

I would like to begin this log by stating that I am very glad to be writing it.

That means I made it back.

Which, at several points during this mission, did not feel guaranteed.

We were sent to retrieve a device.

That part made sense.

We find it.

We bring it back.

We move on to the next thing.

Simple.

It was not simple.

The forest had… rules.

Not written rules.

Not posted signs.

But real ones.

The kind you learn by almost doing the wrong thing.

Or watching someone else who already did.

Kael Thorn made it to the Core.

That part stuck with me.

He wasn't careless.

He wasn't untrained.

He just missed something important.

Actually, probably several important things.

And the forest didn't correct him.

It just… let him continue.

That's what I didn't expect.

There was no moment where something jumped out and stopped us.

No obvious warning.

Just a series of small decisions.

And if you made enough of the wrong ones—

That was it.

We had moments like that.

The river.

The markings.

The plants that looked safe and absolutely were not safe.

The part where something in the forest was quietly deciding whether or not we were worth the effort.

I did not enjoy that part.

At all.

But we made it.

And I think the reason we made it is because we stopped trying to win.

We stopped trying to get through it.

We started trying to understand it.

Also, we stayed together.

Which I highly recommend.

If there is one official lesson I would like to record, it is this:

If you are ever in a forest where everything looks normal but probably isn't—

Do not rush.

Do not assume.

And definitely do not eat anything that looks like a berry unless Lydia tells you it's safe.

That is now a personal rule.

The Core is back.

It did not explode.

We did not break it.

I consider that a success.

We also brought Kael back.

Which matters more.

So overall—

Mission complete.

Lessons learned.

And I am officially adding "protected forests with rules you can't see" to my list of places I would prefer not to revisit immediately.

Eventually?

Maybe.

But next mission—

I'm hoping for something with fewer silent predators and deceptive plants.

That would be nice.

End Log.

Author's Note

There are places in life that do not respond well to urgency.

We are used to solving problems by moving quickly, making decisions, and pressing forward until something changes. In many situations, that works. It is often expected.

But not always.

Some environments—whether they are physical places, relationships, or responsibilities—require something different. They require patience. They require observation. They require a willingness to admit that we may not yet understand what we are facing.

This story explores that idea.

The forest in this book is not dangerous because it is hostile. It is difficult because it cannot be rushed. It does not adjust to those who enter it. Instead, it requires those who enter to adjust themselves.

That is not only true in stories.

It is true in life.

There are moments when strength is shown by action.
And there are moments when strength is shown by restraint.

Learning the difference is not easy.

But it matters.

More than once in this story, success came not from doing more—but from doing less. Not from taking—but from understanding what should be left alone.

That is a lesson worth holding onto.

Thank you for taking this journey with these characters. I hope it leaves you with something to consider the next time you find yourself in a situation that does not respond to speed or certainty.

Some things are not meant to be forced.

They are meant to be understood.

— Russell McFall

Cadet Reference Manual — Eldergreen Assignment

Eldergreen Expanse

A protected planetary forest region governed under sovereign authority. The Expanse is not restricted due to hostility, but due to its complexity, ecological balance, and the presence of long-established tribal territories.

Boundary Line

A clearly marked transition point between controlled territory and the Eldergreen Expanse. The boundary is not a defensive barrier, but a point of decision—entry beyond it requires permission, understanding, and adherence to strict conditions.

Conditional Entry Protocol

Authorization granted under specific behavioral and environmental restrictions. Includes limitations on equipment, movement, interaction with local inhabitants, and prohibition of unnecessary environmental impact.

Environmental Interpretation

The process of understanding terrain, movement, and conditions without relying on fixed maps or instruments. Requires observation, patience, and adaptation rather than assumption.

Non-Linear Navigation

A movement approach that does not rely on fixed paths or direct routes. Progress is achieved through reading terrain patterns, environmental flow, and subtle indicators rather than following a predefined course.

Reference Loss Condition

A state in which standard navigation tools or mapped guidance become unreliable due to environmental variability. Requires transition from mapped navigation to observational interpretation.

Flow-Based Pathing

A navigation method using natural movement patterns such as water flow, terrain slope, and environmental compaction to determine direction. Often more reliable than visual paths in dynamic ecosystems.

Deceptive Growth

Plant life that visually resembles safe or neutral species but produces harmful effects if handled or consumed. Requires verification before interaction. Common within complex ecological systems.

Predator Awareness State

A condition identified by reduced ambient sound and altered movement patterns within the environment. Indicates the presence of a higher-order predator observing or evaluating nearby activity.

Non-Threat Posture

A behavioral approach used to avoid escalation with predators. Includes controlled movement, maintained formation, and avoidance of sudden actions that could trigger pursuit or defensive response.

Cultural Boundary Respect

Recognition and preservation of tribal territories and markers within the Expanse. Includes non-interference, non-collection of artifacts, and avoidance of unintended intrusion.

Artifact Non-Removal Principle

A governing rule prohibiting the removal of objects from their original context unless confirmed to be outside cultural or ecological significance. Prevents unintended disruption of local systems.

Environmental Alignment

The process of adjusting actions, movement, or equipment to match the natural conditions of the environment rather than forcing external structure onto it.

Orientation Drift (Core Condition)

A state in which the Quantum StarPath Core attempts to establish positional reference without proper external inputs. Results in continuous recalibration attempts and unstable operational behavior.

Neutral Baseline Stabilization

A corrective method involving physical leveling and environmental simplification to reduce interference and allow system recalibration. Used to restore partial Core stability.

Interference Misinterpretation

A condition where advanced systems incorrectly interpret natural environmental features as valid operational references, leading to flawed processing outcomes.

Respect-Based Operation
An approach in which success is defined not only by mission completion, but by adherence to environmental, cultural, and situational constraints.

Entry Discipline
The understanding that how a location is entered determines the outcome of the mission. Emphasizes patience, awareness, and restraint at the point of transition.

Exit Degradation Principle
The concept that returning from a complex environment is not equivalent to entry. Conditions may change, paths may disappear, and successful exit requires independent interpretation rather than retracing steps.

Recovered Asset — Quantum StarPath Core
A high-value navigation device capable of deep-space positional alignment. When removed from its intended system environment, the Core remains active but requires stabilization before safe transport.

Recovered Personnel — Kael Thorn
Independent operator who successfully transported the Core into the Expanse but failed to stabilize it or exit the environment. Serves as a case study in incomplete operational understanding.

Primary Lesson — Eldergreen Doctrine

Not all environments are obstacles to overcome. Some are systems to be understood.

Success is achieved not by taking from them, but by learning how to move within them—and leaving them unchanged.

APPENDIX — ELDERGREEN FIELD GUIDE (CADET NOTES)

False Sunberries

Type: Plant

Observed Behavior: Small, bright berries visually similar to safe varieties. Found in clusters within dense undergrowth. Causes rapid dehydration if consumed.

Cadet Note: If it looks safe but hasn't been confirmed, it isn't safe.

River Antelope

Type: Animal

Observed Behavior: Small, fast-moving herbivore commonly found near water sources. Leaves clear hoof tracks along riverbanks.

Cadet Note: Useful for locating water. Do not corner.

Shadowpanther

Type: Predator

Observed Behavior: Silent, territorial hunter. Observes before engaging. Avoids conflict unless provoked or given advantage.

Cadet Note: If the forest goes quiet, you are no longer alone.

Root-Lattice Ground

Type: Terrain

Observed Behavior: Dense root systems create unstable footing. Often concealed beneath a thin soil layer.

Cadet Note: Watch your step—what looks flat rarely is.

Flow Channels (Rain Paths)

Type: Terrain

Observed Behavior: Subtle ground patterns formed by water movement. Visible only under proper angle and lighting.

Cadet Note: Water always finds the right path. Follow it when you can't find your own.

Stone Markers (Non-Tribal)

Type: Artificial Marker

Observed Behavior: Straight-line carvings used for direction. Distinct from native tribal symbols, which are curved and flowing.

Cadet Note: If it's simple and direct, it probably wasn't made by the forest's people.

Canopy Compression Zones

Type: Environmental Condition

Observed Behavior: Areas where dense overhead growth reduces light significantly, altering perception and depth awareness.

Cadet Note: When the light changes, your judgment does too.

Compaction Trails (Directional Movement)

Type: Terrain Indicator

Observed Behavior: Slightly compressed ground caused by repeated movement. Not visible as a clear path—identified through density differences.

Cadet Note: Don't look for the trail—look for what changed.

Slope Shift Indicators

Type: Terrain

Observed Behavior: Subtle changes in ground angle affecting water flow and movement patterns. Often difficult to detect without observation.

Cadet Note: If direction stops making sense, check the ground—not the map.

Stable Ridge Lines

Type: Terrain

Observed Behavior: Elevated ground with firmer soil and reduced environmental shift. Often safer for movement during unstable conditions.

Cadet Note: When the ground fails, go higher.

Low-Growth Containment Zones

Type: Environmental Condition

Observed Behavior: Dense, compact areas with reduced airflow, muted sound, and limited visibility. Often found near cave systems.

Cadet Note: When the forest grows quiet, pay closer attention—not less.

Cave Flow Systems

Type: Terrain Structure

Observed Behavior: Subterranean passages formed by historical water movement. May contain smooth stone surfaces and variable footing.

Cadet Note: What shaped the space before you entered it still matters.

Orientation Drift (Core Interaction)

Type: Technical Condition

Observed Behavior: The Quantum StarPath Core attempts to establish position using incorrect environmental references, resulting in instability.

Cadet Note: If a system doesn't understand where it is, it cannot function correctly.

Neutral Alignment Surface

Type: Technical Method

Observed Behavior: A physically leveled base used to stabilize equipment when proper reference systems are unavailable.

Cadet Note: When nothing makes sense, start by making one thing steady.

Boundary Line Transition

Type: Environmental Threshold

Observed Behavior: Clear division between controlled territory and the Eldergreen Expanse. Marks a shift in required behavior and awareness.

Cadet Note: Crossing the line is easy. Entering the right way is not.

Compiled from Delta Crew field observations during the Eldergreen Retrieval Assignment.

Appendix — Why Some Places Are Protected

The Story of Yellowstone National Park establishment

In 1872, something remarkable happened.

A large stretch of land in the western United States—filled with geysers, rivers, forests, and wildlife—was set aside and protected. Not for farming. Not for mining. Not for ownership.

But for preservation.

That land became known as Yellowstone National Park—**the first national park in the world**.

At the time, this was a new idea.

For generations, land had been something people used, claimed, or changed. If something valuable was found—timber, minerals, or fertile ground—it was expected that it would be taken and developed.

But Yellowstone was different.

The people who explored it saw something they did not fully understand.

Geysers that erupted without warning.

Hot springs that shimmered with unusual colors.

Vast herds of animals moving through wide valleys.

Forests that seemed to operate on their own quiet rhythms.

It was beautiful.

But it was also complex.

And instead of trying to control it, a decision was made:

Leave it as it is.

Protect it.

Allow people to see it—but not to take it.

A Different Kind of Thinking

That decision changed more than just one place.

It introduced a new idea—one that was not always easy to follow:

Some places are not meant to be changed.

Not because they are fragile.

But because they are complete.

Yellowstone did not need improvement.

It needed understanding.

Visitors could walk through it.

Study it.

Learn from it.

But they were asked to do so carefully.

Stay on marked paths.

Do not disturb wildlife.

Do not remove what you find.

These rules were not there to limit people.

They were there to protect something larger than any one person's experience.

Learning the Right Way to Enter

Over time, people discovered something important.

The danger in Yellowstone was not always obvious.

Hot springs could look calm—but be dangerously hot.

Wild animals could seem peaceful—but react quickly if approached.

The land itself could shift in ways that were not easy to predict.

The problem was not that Yellowstone was unsafe.

The problem was assuming it behaved like other places.

Those who respected it learned how to move within it safely.

Those who ignored its nature often found themselves in trouble—not because the land acted against them, but because they misunderstood it.

What Yellowstone Teaches

Yellowstone still stands today.

Largely unchanged.

Still protected.

Still teaching the same lesson.

Not everything valuable is meant to be taken.

Some things are meant to be experienced, understood, and left as they are.

The boundaries around Yellowstone are not there to keep people out.

They are there to remind us:

Entering a place like this requires something different.

Patience.

Awareness.

Respect.

A Lesson That Still Matters

In many ways, Yellowstone represents a shift in how we see the world.

It reminds us that strength is not always found in control.

Sometimes, it is found in restraint.

In knowing when to step carefully.

In knowing when not to interfere.

And in understanding that some systems—natural or otherwise—are already working exactly as they should.

We do not improve them by taking from them.

We learn from them by moving within them the right way.

Some places are protected not because they are dangerous…
but because they are worth understanding before they are touched.

Reflection 1 — The Earth Is Not Ours

"The earth is the Lord's, and all it contains,
The world, and those who dwell in it." — Psalm 24:1 (NASB)

It is easy to think of the world as something given to us to use.
And in many ways, it is.
We build.
We grow.
We create.
But this verse reminds us of something deeper.
We are not owners.
We are stewards.
There is a difference.
An owner takes what he wants.
A steward cares for what has been entrusted to him.

Places like Yellowstone help us see that more clearly. They stand as reminders that not everything is placed before us to be used or changed. Some things are given to us so that we might learn how to care for them—and, at times, how to leave them as they are.

That kind of thinking does not come naturally.
It must be learned.
And once learned, it shapes how we see everything else.

Reflection 2 — Wisdom Walks Carefully

"See then that you walk carefully, not as unwise but as wise."
— Ephesians 5:15 (NASB)

There are places where moving quickly works.
And there are places where it does not.
The difference is not always obvious at first.
That is why this verse matters.
"Walk carefully" does not mean walk fearfully.
It means walk with awareness.
With attention.
With the willingness to observe before acting.
In a place like Yellowstone, that kind of wisdom keeps people safe.
In life, it does something even greater.
It keeps us from assuming we understand something we have only just encountered.

It slows us down just enough to recognize that not every situation is meant to be handled the same way.

Some require strength.
Some require patience.
And some require the humility to realize—
We are still learning where we are.

Some places teach us how to move.
Others teach us how to slow down.
The wise learn the difference.

Character Recap — Quick Guide

Richard Taylor

Team leader. Calm and steady, Richard helps the group make good decisions—especially when things aren't clear.

Ashton Quinn

Operations specialist. Ashton understands how things work and often notices patterns others miss.

Dooley Lewis

Engineer. Dooley keeps equipment working and solves problems with practical thinking (and a little humor).

Milo Santiago

Data specialist. Milo pays close attention to small details and often sees changes before anyone else.

Princess Lydia

Guide to the forest. Lydia understands the Eldergreen Expanse and teaches the team how to move through it the right way.

Serana

Royal guardian. Serana protects Lydia and the team with quiet focus and careful awareness.

Kael Thorn

Explorer who came before the team. He reached the objective—but didn't fully understand the dangers along the way.

Mother

Ship AI. Mother runs the ship systems and only reports what can be clearly measured.

Whizzy

Small helper AI. Whizzy watches closely and notices important details others might miss.

ABOUT THE SERIES

Living in the Delta Era

The Delta Era is no longer theoretical.
It has become a way of operating.

What once felt like preparation has settled into practice. The cadets now work in a reality where certainty is rare, clarity often arrives too late to guide decisions, and success cannot always be measured by what was fixed or prevented.

Systems still function.
Procedures still matter.

But experience has taught them that not every outcome can be traced, documented, or explained.

Some missions end without answers.
Some dangers dissolve instead of advancing.
And some of the most important moments leave no record beyond the judgment of those who were present.

In this phase of the series, growth is no longer measured by promotion, recognition, or visible success. It is measured by discernment. The cadets learn when action is required—and when restraint is the greater responsibility. They discover that leadership often means carrying unresolved questions, and choosing not to share risks others are not ready to bear.

The Delta Era explores a deeper truth:
that faithfulness is not always rewarded with understanding, and responsibility does not always arrive with permission.

These stories continue to value courage, loyalty, and friendship—but they place them under quieter pressures. Trust must coexist with caution. Authority must be exercised without certainty. Integrity must hold even when outcomes cannot be publicly justified or fully known.

The missions grow more complex not because the universe is louder—
but because it has learned how to remain silent.

The 7-Second Signal marked the threshold.
The stories that followed confirmed the change.

This book affirms what the Delta Era has become.

In this mission, the lesson is not how to overcome an environment—but how to enter it correctly. Not every objective is meant to be taken. Some must be approached with restraint, understood with patience, and left unchanged except for what must be responsibly returned.

From here forward, the cadets operate in a universe where listening matters as much as action, where restoring responsibility can matter more than providing solutions, and where the most meaningful victories may never be claimed—or even seen.

The Delta Era is not about what is revealed.
It is about what is recognized—
and responsibly left in the right hands.

About the Author

Russell McFall writes thoughtful, character-driven science fiction that explores leadership, responsibility, and the quiet decisions that shape a life.

Before becoming a full-time writer, Russell spent many years in software development, where clear thinking and problem-solving were part of everyday work. Alongside that career, he and his wife devoted years to children's ministry and homeschooling their family—experiences that continue to influence the heart and direction of his stories.

Many of his books began as bedtime adventures for his children. Those early stories grew into the *Space Cadet Legacy* series, where readers follow young cadets learning not only how to navigate space, but how to lead, listen, and act with wisdom under pressure.

Russell writes with a focus on clean, meaningful storytelling that can be enjoyed by both younger readers and adults. His work emphasizes teamwork, integrity, and the importance of doing what is right—even when the outcome is uncertain.

He continues to write with the same sense of wonder that inspired those first stories many years ago.

Also by Russell McFall

Ordained Path Books

Clean Science Fiction and Inspirational Writing for Thoughtful Readers

---

Contemporary Fiction and Short Stories

Stories of Community, Memory, and Hope

- **Squirrel Creek Estates — Where the Porch Lights Stay On**
- **The World That Chose**

The Space Cadet Richard Series

Where the Legacy Began

- **The Final Countdown**
- **The Dunes of Dinkytown**
- **The Mastermind's Maze**

The Space Cadet Legacy Series

Over 30+ novels of courage, friendship, and discovery — including

- **The First Gate**
- **Welcome Back, Player**
- **Flibber's Journey Home**
- **Stronger Together**
- **Phasegate Rising**
- **The Makers' Handshake**

(New missions continuing.)

Literary Humor and Reflections

Serious Nonsense — Sanity Sold Separately

Devotional and Reflection Books

- **Remembering God's Help — Stone by Stone**
- **Attributes of God**
- **This Is My Story, This Is My Song**
- **Lives of Faith**
- **Foundations of Faith**

Russell McFall writes clean fiction and thoughtful reflections designed to uplift the heart, sharpen the mind, and remind every reader that light still wins.

www.ingramcontent.com/pod-product-compliance
Lightning Source LLC
LaVergne TN
LVHW010640110826
845149LV00014B/2906

* 9 7 8 1 9 7 2 7 2 4 0 8 8 *